序　言

　　教育部專款補助「財團法人語言訓練測驗中心」，推行「全民英語能力分級檢定測驗」後，預計在未來，所有國小、國中學生，以及一般社會人士，如計程車駕駛、百貨業、餐飲業、旅遊業或觀光景點服務人員、維修技術人員、一般行政助理等，均須通過「初級英語能力檢定測驗」，以作為畢業、就業、升遷時之英語能力證明，已是必然趨勢，此項測驗的重要性，可見一斑。

　　繼「初級英語聽力檢定①②」之後，我們再推出「初級英檢模擬試題①②」，完全仿照「初級英語能力檢定測驗」中的題型，書中囊括聽力測驗、閱讀能力測驗，以及寫作能力測驗，希望能幫助讀者輕鬆通過初級檢定的初試測驗。本書試題全部經過劉毅英文「初級英語檢定模考班」，實際在課堂上使用過，效果奇佳。本書所有試題均附有詳細的中文翻譯及單字註解，節省讀者查字典的時間。同時，這些珍貴的試題，也有助於國中同學準備基本學力測驗及第二階段考試。

　　感謝這麼多讀者，給我們鼓勵。編輯好書，是「學習」一貫的宗旨，讀者若需要任何學習英文的書，都可以提供意見給我們，我們的目標是，學英文的書，「學習」都有；「學習」出版、天天進步。也盼望讀者們不吝給我們批評指正。

編者　謹識

本書製作過程

感謝劉毅英文「初級英語檢定模考班」的同學們，在上課的八週期間，提供許多寶貴的意見，讓這些試題更加完善。感謝美籍老師 Laura E. Stewart 負責校訂，也要感謝林愔予小姐協助編寫聽力詳解，以及謝靜芳老師再三仔細校訂，白雪嬌小姐負責封面設計，李佩姍小姐繪製插圖，洪淑娟小姐及王淑平小姐協助完稿，黃淑貞小姐負責版面設計及打字。

全民英語能力分級檢定測驗
初級測驗①

一、聽力測驗

　　本測驗分三部份，全爲三選一之選擇題，每部份各 10 題，共 30 題，作答時間約 20 分鐘。

第一部份：看圖辨義

　　　　本部份共 10 題，試題冊上每題有一個圖片，請聽錄音機播出一個相關的問題，與 A、B、C 三個英語敘述後，選一個與所看到圖片最相符的答案，並在答案紙上相對的圓圈內塗黑作答。每題播出一遍，問題及選項均不印在試題冊上。

例：（看）

NT$80　　NT$50

（聽）

Look at the picture.　How much is the hamburger?

　　A.　It's eighty dollars.
　　B.　It's fifty-five dollars.
　　C.　It's eighteen dollars.

正確答案爲 A

Question 1

Question 2

Question 3

Question 4

Question 5

Question 6

請 翻 頁 ⫸

Question 7

Question 8

Question 9

Question 10

請 翻 頁 ▯▯⟹

第二部份：問答

本部份共 10 題，每題錄音機會播出一個問句或直述句，每題播出一次，聽後請從試題冊上 A、B、C 三個選項中，選出一個最適合的回答或回應，並在答案紙上塗黑作答。

例：

（聽） Good morning, Kevin. How are you?

（看） A.　I'm fine, thank you.
　　　 B.　I'm in the living room.
　　　 C.　My name is Kevin.

正確答案為 A

11. A. My sister is the one in the yellow coat.
　　B. She looks just like my sister.
　　C. I can't see him.

12. A. How would you like your steak?
　　B. Is that for here or to go?
　　C. Are you hungry?

13. A. The shoes are on the floor.
　　B. The third floor.
　　C. You can take the elevator.

14. A. Put it on before you go outside.
　　B. Put it down; it's not yours.
　　C. Put it on the chair.

15. A. Two years ago.
　　B. At school.
　　C. No, I haven't.

16. A. I am usually late for school.
　　B. I do my homework before school.
　　C. I take my dog to the park.

17. A. No, I don't.
　　B. My name is Bob.
　　C. Mary is her name.

18. A. Once upon a time…
　　B. It's an English novel.
　　C. Because I have a test tomorrow.

19. A. In about 15 minutes.
　　B. At the main station.
　　C. Today is Tuesday.

20. A. She wasn't badly hurt.
　　B. She was bad.
　　C. She was climbing a tree.

請 翻 頁 ⟹

第三部份：簡短對話

本部份共 10 題，每題錄音機會播出一段對話及一個相關的問題，每題播出兩次，聽後請從試題冊上 A、B、C 三個選項中，選出一個最適合的回答，並在答案紙上塗黑作答。

例：

（聽） (Woman) Good afternoon, ...Mr. Davis?

(Man) Yes. I have an appointment with Dr. Sanders at two o'clock. My son Tommy has a fever.

(Woman) Oh, that's too bad. Well, please have a seat, Mr. Davis. Dr. Sanders will be right with you.

Question: Where did this conversation take place?

（看） A. In a post office.

B. In a restaurant.

C. In a doctor's office.

正確答案為 C

21. A. He is going with the woman.

B. He is going to a shopping mall.

C. He is going right now.

22. A. She is going to the train station.

B. She is going by taxi.

C. She is going to the airport.

23. A. Play a musical
       instrument.
    B. Do his homework.
    C. Go to a movie.

24. A. It is on the corner.
    B. It is closed now.
    C. We don't know.

25. A. On the telephone.
    B. In a restaurant.
    C. In the school cafeteria.

26. A. Take the pen back to
       the store.
    B. Turn the pen around.
    C. Write with a new pen.

27. A. In about six hours.
    B. In a car.
    C. Very quickly.

28. A. She and the woman
       share the room now.
    B. She is older than the
       woman.
    C. She doesn't like to
       read.

29. A. He usually goes to
       school by taxi.
    B. He usually takes the
       school bus.
    C. He often misses the
       school bus.

30. A. She took some
       medicine.
    B. She has a cold.
    C. She doesn't like the
       doctor.

請 翻 頁

二、閱讀能力測驗

本測驗分三部份，全爲四選一之選擇題，共 35 題，作答時間 35 分鐘。

第一部份：詞彙和結構

本部份共 15 題，每題含一個空格。請就試題冊上 A、B、C、D 四個選項中選出最適合題意的字或詞，標示在答案紙上。

1. Irene made up her mind to go _____ a diet because she put on five kilograms during her vacation in the U.S.
   A. to
   B. in
   C. up
   D. on

2. You may take _____ your coat if you feel hot.
   A. on
   B. of
   C. off
   D. in

3. The basketball player _____ the ball to her teammate.
   A. shouted
   B. passed
   C. ran
   D. spread

4. Paula says the party will be _____, so she suggests we wear casual clothes, like jeans.
   A. informal
   B. serious
   C. sad
   D. wonderful

5. Sid laughed _____ when I told him the joke. Everyone in the classroom could hear his laughter.
   A. loudly
   B. secretly
   C. strongly
   D. weakly

6. Becky _____ herself an orange juice in the café before her friends arrive.
   A. changes
   B. orders
   C. moves
   D. waits

7. Helen studies in a bilingual school. She _____ there since she was 6 years old.
   A. is
   B. was
   C. has been
   D. have been

請 翻 頁 ⫸

8. The weather in summer is not _____ hot but also wet.
It's hard to imagine studying in a classroom without an
air conditioner.
A. very
B. that
C. only
D. less

9. The cafeteria was full, but Kevin saw an empty seat next
to his classmate. "_____ I sit there?" Kevin asked his
classmate.
A. Should
B. May
C. Would
D. Will

10. Learning a second language _____ not as easy as you think.
A. is
B. are
C. which is
D. which are

11. Nick, no one can help you with this problem. You should
try to solve it by _____.
A. you
B. yours
C. yourself
D. yourselves

12. Paul will drive his car and Mandy will drive _____.
    A. her
    B. hers
    C. your
    D. my

13. Please look before crossing the road and _____ across
    the street quickly.
    A. walk
    B. walks
    C. to walk
    D. walking

14. Jessie has two sons; one works in the post office, and
    _____ works in the hospital.
    A. both
    B. another
    C. the one
    D. the other

15. Matt and Jen usually _____ to the library after school,
    but they didn't go there today.
    A. were going
    B. will go
    C. went
    D. go

請 翻 頁 ⫸

第二部份：段落填空
　　　　本部份共 10 題，包括二個段落，每個段落各含 5 個空格。
　　　　請就試題冊上 A、B、C、D 四個選項中選出最適合題意
　　　　的字或詞，標示在答案紙上。

Questions 16-20

　　Dogs have been man's good friend for thousands of years. There are many ___(16)___ about brave dogs helping people in danger. ___(17)___ their help, many people lost in the mountains found their way home. Dogs can be stars, too. A dog called Lassie was the star of a popular ___(18)___.

　　Dogs can hear and smell better than man, but they can't see so ___(19)___. A dog lives about 12 or 13 years. A ___(20)___ child has not grown up yet, but a dog of that age is very old.

16. A. stories
　　B. zoos
　　C. pictures
　　D. opportunities

17. A. For
　　B. Without
　　C. With
　　D. From

18. A. store
　　B. movie
　　C. restaurant
　　D. computer

19. A. clear
　　B. nice
　　C. well
　　D. better

20. A. thirteen years old
　　B. thirteen-years-old
　　C. thirteen-year-old
　　D. thirteen year-old

Questions 21-25

Scott and I agreed to meet ___(21)___ 8:00 this morning, but he didn't show up until 9:00. "I've been waiting here for an hour," I said. "This is the third ___(22)___ you've been late for this month." Then I asked him if he was sorry, but he shook his head. "So I was late," he said. "So what?" Then he walked away. Since then, I ___(23)___ very upset. In fact, I'm not sure I can be Scott's friend anymore. I ___(24)___ I'll go over to his house and ___(25)___ him that now.

21. A. at
    B. in
    C. on
    D. for

22. A. chance
    B. appointment
    C. question
    D. review

23. A. has been
    B. have been
    C. was
    D. were

24. A. thought
    B. thinks
    C. think
    D. thinking

25. A. telling
    B. told
    C. to tell
    D. tell

請 翻 頁 ⫸

第三部份：閱讀理解

　　　　　本部份共 10 題，包括數段短文，每段短文後有 1～3 個相
　　　　　關問題，請就試題冊上 A、B、C、D 四個選項中選出最
　　　　　適合者，標示在答案紙上。

Questions 26-27

What	: "P" Party
Why	: To celebrate Rachel's moving into a new house
When	: August 9, Friday night, at 9:00
Where	: Rachel's new house
How	: Play any role that starts with the letter "P"

26. The party will be held _____.
    A. on Friday morning
    B. at Rachel's new house
    C. for Rachel's birthday
    D. in September

27. Which is true?
    A. Rachel is giving the party to say good-bye to her friends.
    B. You can dress as a "teacher" or a "turtle."
    C. You can dress as a "pizza deliveryman" or a "potato."
    D. Anyone who goes to the party must bring his own food.

Questions 28-29

GOOD MORNING!

This is Ms. Kelly's English 1 class
at Burlington Elementary School.

Today is Wednesday, Sept. 9.

CLASS RULES

1. Be on time for class.
2. Raise your hand to answer a question.
3. Pay attention to your teacher.
4. Do your homework.

28. Who is the teacher?
   A. Ms. Kelly.
   B. Mr. Kelly.
   C. Ms. Stewart.
   D. Mr. Stewart.

29. The English teacher doesn't want her students
   A. to raise their hands to answer questions.
   B. to wear casual clothes in class.
   C. to be late for class.
   D. to do their assignments.

請 翻 頁 ⫸

Questions 30-32

Dear Ann,

My problem is my father is never home. He is a sales representative, and he is always going to the airport, or the train station, or the bus station. He is working in Kaohsiung this week. Next week he is going to Hualien. When my father *is* at home, he is tired, or he is working in his office. What can I do?

Lonely Son in Taipei

30. What's the boy's problem?
    A. His father lost his job.
    B. His father and mother don't love each other.
    C. His father is afraid to take the plane.
    D. His father works hard and spends little time with him.

31. What is his father going to do next week?

    A. He is going to the U.S. on business.

    B. He is going to have a holiday in Hualien with his children.

    C. He is going to Hualien to sell the goods of his company.

    D. He is going to stay in Taipei and spend the whole week with his family.

32. The word "lonely" in line nine means _____.

    A. unhappy

    B. excited

    C. outgoing

    D. hungry

請 翻 頁 ⫸

Questions 33-35

　　Children and grownups enjoy playing with kites. There are a lot of kite festivals and competitions in China and many other countries. But kites are not just playthings. They can be useful in many other ways.

　　Kite flying has been popular in China for more than two thousand years. Scientists have been interested in kites for a long time. They have used them for studying the weather and for testing new kinds of flying machines. Today scientists have created many new kinds of kites. Some of these can pull boats or lift a man easily.

　　Some kites are really beautiful works of art. People are interested in kites because kite flying is both an art and a science. Most important of all, it is fun.

33. Kites are enjoyed by _____.
    A. children
    B. adults
    C. only children and adults in China
    D. people of all ages in many countries

34. People have NOT used kites for _____.

    A. knowing the changes in weather

    B. a way of traveling from country to country

    C. studying new machines

    D. a fun activity in their free time

35. People are interested in kites because _____.

    A. kites are expensive

    B. kites are useful in science

    C. kite flying is a good exercise

    D. kites were invented by the Chinese

請 翻 頁 ⅢⅢ⟹

三、寫作能力測驗

　　本測驗共有兩部份，第一部份爲單句寫作，第二部份爲段落寫作。測驗時間爲 40 分鐘。

第一部份：單句寫作

　　　　　　請將答案寫在寫作能力測驗答案紙對應的題號旁，如有拼字、標點、大小寫之錯誤，將予扣分。

第 1～5 題：句子改寫

　　　　　　請依題目之提示，將原句改寫成指定型式，並將改寫的句子完整地寫在答案紙上（包括提示之文字及標點符號）。

1. Jerry　: Did you bring the comic book?

   Carrie : Oh, I forgot.

   Carrie forgot _____ the comic book.

2. My backpack is different from yours. （用 the same as）

   _____.

3. When is the next movie?

   Tell us when _____.

4. To keep a pet is not easy.

   It _____.

5. Mandy went to the gift shop.

   Why _____ the gift shop?

第 6～10 題：句子合併

　　　　請依照題目指示，將兩句合併成一句，並將合併的句子
　　　　完整地寫在答案紙上（包括提示之文字及標點符號）。

6. Patricia told Joyce something.

   John went home late.

   Patricia told Joyce why _____.

7. I have a dog.

   My dog is sleeping right now.

   I have a dog that _____.

8. We moved the piano.

   My neighbors helped us.

   My neighbors helped us _____.

9. I went to the Museum of Fine Arts.

   I took the bus there.

   I went _____ by _____.

10. Linda is very old.

    Linda cannot see well.

    Linda is too old _____.

請 翻 頁 ▯▯⟹

第 11～15 題：重組

　　　　請將題目中所有提示字詞整合成一有意義的句子，並
　　　　將重組的句子完整地寫在答案紙上（包括提示之文字
　　　　及標點符號）。答案中必須使用所有提示字詞，且不
　　　　能隨意增加字詞，否則不予計分。

11. Would _____.
　　 like / tea / cup / you / to have / a / of

12. Nancy _____.
　　 most / questions / can / difficult / the / answer

13. The weather _____.
　　 so / I / stay / that / is / hot / would rather / inside

14. Paul _____.
　　 has / sick / for / a / been / month

15. Kay _____.
　　 afraid / taking / tests / is / of / English / not

第二部份：段落寫作

題目：請根據圖片內容寫一篇約 50 字的簡短描述。

初級英檢模擬試題①詳解

一、聽力測驗

第一部份

Look at the picture for question 1.

1. (**A**) How does he eat his noodles?
   A. He eats them with a fork.
   B. He eats them with a spoon.
   C. He eats them with chopsticks.

   * noodle (ˈnudḷ) n. 麵條　　fork (fɔrk) n. 叉子
   spoon (spun) n. 湯匙
   chopsticks (ˈtʃɑpˌstɪks) n. pl. 筷子

Look at the picture for question 2.

2. (**B**) What class does he teach?
   A. Medicine.　　　　　　B. Chemistry.
   C. PE.

   * medicine (ˈmɛdəsn̩) n. 醫學
   chemistry (ˈkɛmɪstrɪ) n. 化學
   PE 體育 (= *physical education*)

Look at the picture for question 3.

3. (**C**) What is he doing?
   A. He is planting a tree.
   B. He is watering the flowers.
   C. He is gardening.

   * plant (plænt) v. 種植　　water (ˈwɔtɚ) v. 澆水
   garden (ˈgɑrdn̩) v. 從事園藝活動

Look at the picture for question 4.

4. (**C**) What does the man in the tower do?
   A. He is an astronomer.
   B. He is a sailor.
   C. He is a lighthouse keeper.

   * ***What does sb. do?*** 某人從事什麼工作？
     tower (ˈtaʊɚ) *n.* 塔
     astronomer (əˈstrɑnəmɚ) *n.* 天文學家
     sailor (ˈselɚ) *n.* 水手；船員
     lighthouse (ˈlaɪt͵haʊs) *n.* 燈塔
     keeper (ˈkipɚ) *n.* 守衛；管理員

Look at the picture for question 5.

5. (**B**) What is the mother bird doing?
   A. She is running after her chicks.
   B. She is flying in circles.
   C. She is feeding her young.

   * ***mother bird*** 母鳥；母雞　　***run after*** 追趕
     chick (tʃɪk) *n.* 小鳥；小雞　　fly (flaɪ) *v.* 飛
     circle (ˈsɝkl̩) *n.* 圓圈　　feed (fid) *v.* 餵食
     young (jʌŋ) *n.* 幼小動物

Look at the picture for question 6.

6. (**B**) Where are they?
   A. They are in a music class.
   B. They are at a dance party.
   C. They are at a funeral.

   * ***dance party*** 舞會　　funeral (ˈfjunərəl) *n.* 葬禮

Look at the picture for question 7.

7. (**C**) What are the people in the cars doing?

    A. They are having an accident.

    B. They are taking a train.

    C. They are enjoying a ride.

    * accident〔'æksədənt〕 *n.* 意外
    ride〔raɪd〕 *n.* 搭乘

Look at the picture for question 8.

8. (**A**) What kind of movie is it?

    A. It is a love story.

    B. It is a comedy.

    C. It is a nature program.

    * kind〔kaɪnd〕 *n.* 種類   *love story* 愛情故事
    comedy〔'kɑmədɪ〕 *n.* 喜劇   nature〔'netʃɚ〕 *n.* 大自然
    nature program 以報導大自然為主題的節目

Look at the picture for question 9.

9. (**A**) Where are the children?

    A. They are at the park.

    B. They are at the airport.

    C. They are in the toy store.

    * airport〔'ɛr͵port〕 *n.* 機場
    toy store 玩具店

Look at the picture for question 10.

10. (**A**) What is he wearing?

      A. He is wearing a tie.

      B. He is wearing a hat.

      C. He is wearing a mirror.

      * wear〔wɛr〕v. 穿；戴   tie〔taɪ〕n. 領帶

        hat〔hæt〕n. 帽子   mirror〔'mɪrɚ〕n. 鏡子

第二部份

11. (**A**) Which girl is your sister?

      A. My sister is the one in the yellow coat.

      B. She looks just like my sister.

      C. I can't see him.

      * yellow〔'jɛlo〕adj. 黃色的   coat〔kot〕n. 外套

12. (**B**) Two hamburgers and two Cokes, please.

      A. How would you like your steak?

      B. Is that for here or to go?

      C. Are you hungry?

      * hamburger〔'hæmbɝgɚ〕n. 漢堡

        Coke〔kok〕n. 可口可樂 (= *Coca-cola*)

        steak〔stek〕n. 牛排

        How would you like your steak? 您的牛排要幾分熟？

        for here 內用   ***to go*** 外帶

        hungry〔'hʌŋgrɪ〕adj. 飢餓的

13. (**B**) Which floor is the shoe department on?

    A. The shoes are on the floor.

    B. The third floor.

    C. You can take the elevator.

    * floor〔flor〕*n.* 樓層；地板　　shoe〔ʃu〕*n.* 鞋子
    department〔dɪˋpɑrtmənt〕*n.* 部門
    take〔tek〕*v.* 搭乘　　elevator〔ˋɛlə͵vetɚ〕*n.* 電梯

14. (**C**) Where can I put my coat?

    A. Put it on before you go outside.

    B. Put it down; it's not yours.

    C. Put it on the chair.

    * put〔put〕*v.* 放　　***put on*** 穿上 (↔ *take off*)
    outside〔ˋautˋsaɪd〕*adv.* 在外面　　***put down*** 放下

15. (**A**) When did you meet Grace?

    A. Two years ago.

    B. At school.

    C. No, I haven't.

    * meet〔mit〕*v.* 認識

16. (**C**) What do you usually do after school?

    A. I am usually late for school.

    B. I do my homework before school.

    C. I take my dog to the park.

    * ***after school*** 放學後　　late〔let〕*adj.* 遲到的

17. (**A**) Do you know that boy's name?

      A. No, I don't.

      B. My name is Bob.

      C. Mary is her name.

18. (**B**) What are you reading?

      A. Once upon a time…

      B. It's an English novel.

      C. Because I have a test tomorrow.

     * ***once upon a time*** 很久很久以前 (故事的開頭語)

      novel〔'nɑvḷ〕*n.* 小說   test〔tɛst〕*n.* 測驗；小考

19. (**A**) When will we arrive in Taipei?

      A. In about 15 minutes.

      B. At the main station.

      C. Today is Tuesday.

     * arrive〔ə'raɪv〕*v.* 到達

      in about 15 minutes 大約再過十五分鐘

      main〔men〕*adj.* 主要的；最大的

20. (**C**) What was your sister doing when she got hurt?

      A. She wasn't badly hurt.

      B. She was bad.

      C. She was climbing a tree.

     * ***get hurt*** 受傷   badly〔'bædlɪ〕*adv.* 嚴重地

      climb〔klaɪm〕*v.* 爬   tree〔tri〕*n.* 樹

第三部份

21. (**B**) W：Where are you going?

M：I'm going to the new mall.

W：Oh. Are you going shopping?

M：No, I'm going to see a movie.

Question：Where is the man going?

A. He is going with the woman.

B. He is going to a shopping mall.

C. He is going right now.

* mall〔mɔl〕*n.* 購物中心（= *shopping mall*）

see a movie 看電影

right now 現在（= *now*）

22. (**C**) M：When are you leaving?

W：My flight is at 10:00.

M：You'd better hurry.

W：It's all right. I can take a taxi there.

Question：Where is the woman going?

A. She is going to the train station.

B. She is going by taxi.

C. She is going to the airport.

* leave〔liv〕*v.* 離開　　flight〔flaɪt〕*n.* 班機

had better + 原形 *V.* 最好

hurry〔'hɝɪ〕*v.* 趕快　　***all right*** 沒問題

taxi〔'tæksɪ〕*n.* 計程車

23. (**A**) M : What are you doing this afternoon?

W : I'm going to a movie with my sister. Would you like to come, too?

M : I'd like to, but I have band practice this afternoon.

Question : What will the boy do this afternoon?

A. Play a musical instrument.

B. Do his homework.

C. Go to a movie.

* ***go to a movie*** 去看電影

would like to V. 想要 (= *want to V.*)

band〔bænd〕*n.* 樂團;樂隊

practice〔'præktɪs〕*n.* 練習　　***musical instrument*** 樂器

24. (**C**) M : Excuse me, do you know where the Whole Grain Bakery is?

W : I'm sorry. I don't know that one, but there's another bakery on the corner.

M : Thanks. I'll just go there.

Question : Where is the Whole Grain Bakery?

A. It is on the corner.

B. It is closed now.

C. We don't know.

* whole〔hol〕*adj.* 完整的　　grain〔gren〕*n.* 穀類

whole grain 雜糧 (麵包)

bakery〔'bekərɪ〕*n.* 麵包店

corner〔'kɔrnɚ〕*n.* 轉角　　close〔kloz〕*v.* 關閉

25. (**B**) W : Good evening. How many, please?

        M : Four. And we'd like to sit in the non-smoking section.

        W : Fine. Follow me.

        Question : Where did this conversation take place?

        A. On the telephone.

        B. In a restaurant.

        C. In the school cafeteria.

        * non-smoking〔nɑn'smokɪŋ〕*adj.* 非吸煙的
section〔'sɛkʃən〕*n.* 區域　　follow〔'falo〕*v.* 跟隨
conversation〔͵kɑnvɚ'seʃən〕*n.* 對話
take place 發生　　cafeteria〔͵kæfə'tɪrɪə〕*n.* 自助餐廳

26. (**A**) W : What's the matter?

        M : I just bought this pen yesterday, and now it won't write.

        W : You should return it.

        Question : What does the girl think the boy should do?

        A. Take the pen back to the store.

        B. Turn the pen around.

        C. Write with a new pen.

        * ***What's the matter?*** 怎麼了？（= *What's wrong?*）
it won't write 它不能寫（= *the pen won't write*）
return〔rɪ'tɝn〕*v.* 退回（= *take back*）
turn around 旋轉

27. (**B**) M：What time will you arrive in Hualien?

W：We are driving, so we'll get there about five.

M：How long is the drive?

W：It takes about six hours.

Question：How will the woman get to Hualien?

A. In about six hours.

B. In a car.

C. Very quickly.

* ***Hualien*** 花蓮　　drive〔draɪv〕*v.* 開車　*n.* 車程
we'll get there about five 我們大約五點鐘會到那裡
How long~? ~（時間）多久？
take〔tek〕*v.* 花費（時間）
quickly〔'kwɪklɪ〕*adv.* 快地

28. (**B**) M：You have a lot of books for a junior high student!

W：Oh, they aren't all mine.　Some are my sister's.

M：Do you share a room with her?

W：Not now.　She is away at college.

Question：What do we know about the girl's sister?

A. She and the woman share the room now.

B. She is older than the woman.

C. She doesn't like to read.

* share〔ʃɛr〕*v.* 分享；共用
away〔ə'we〕*adv.* 不在
college〔'kɑlɪdʒ〕*n.* 大學
read〔rid〕*v.* 閱讀

29. (**B**) W : Why are you so late today?

M : I missed the school bus.

W : Did you come by taxi?

M : No, I took a city bus.

Question : How does the boy usually get to school?

A. He usually goes to school by taxi.

B. He usually takes the school bus.

C. He often misses the school bus.

* miss〔mɪs〕v. 錯過　　***school bus*** 校車

city bus 市公車　　usually〔'juʒʊəlɪ〕adv. 通常

30. (**B**) M : You look awful.

W : I have a cold.

M : Why don't you go see a doctor?

W : Because I hate to take medicine.

Question : Why does the girl look awful?

A. She took some medicine.

B. She has a cold.

C. She doesn't like the doctor.

* awful〔'ɔful, 'ɔfl̩〕adj. 可怕的；糟糕的

have a cold 感冒（= *catch a cold*）

hate〔het〕v. 討厭　　medicine〔'mɛdəsn̩〕n. 藥

take medicine 吃藥

二、閱讀能力測驗

第一部份：詞彙和結構

1. (**D**) Irene made up her mind to go <u>on</u> a diet because she put on five kilograms during her vacation in the U.S.
艾琳下定決心要<u>節食</u>，因爲她在美國渡假期間，胖了五公斤。

> ***go on a diet*** 節食

* ***make up*** one's ***mind*** + ***to V.*** 下定決心~　　***put on*** 增加
kilogram〔'kɪlə,græm〕*n.* 公斤 (= *kg* = *kilo*)
during〔'djʊrɪŋ〕*prep.* 在…期間
vacation〔ve'keʃən〕*n.* 假期

2. (**C**) You may take <u>off</u> your coat if you feel hot.
如果你覺得熱的話，你可以<u>脫掉</u>外套。

> ***take off*** 脫掉 (↔ *put on*)

* coat〔kot〕*n.* 外套

3. (**B**) The basketball player <u>passed</u> the ball to her teammate.
那名籃球選手把球<u>傳</u>給她的隊友。

(A) shout〔ʃaʊt〕*v.* 大叫
(B) ***pass***〔pæs〕*v.* 傳遞
(C) run〔rʌn〕*v.* 跑
(D) spread〔sprɛd〕*v.* 攤開

* player〔'pleɚ〕*n.* 選手
teammate〔'tim,met〕*n.* 隊友

4. (**A**) Paula says the party will be <u>informal</u>, so she suggests we wear casual clothes, like jeans. 寶拉說這會是個<u>非正式的</u>宴會，所以她建議我們穿著便服，像是牛仔褲。

 (A) ***informal*** 〔ɪnˋfɔrml〕*adj.* 非正式的；不拘禮儀的

 (B) serious 〔ˋsɪrɪəs〕*adj.* 嚴肅的

 (C) sad 〔sæd〕*adj.* 難過的

 (D) wonderful 〔ˋwʌndəfəl〕*adj.* 很棒的

 * suggest 〔səˋdʒɛst〕*v.* 建議
  casual 〔ˋkæʒʊəl〕*adj.*（服裝等）非正式的
  jeans 〔dʒinz〕*n. pl.* 牛仔褲

5. (**A**) Sid laughed <u>loudly</u> when I told him the joke. Everyone in the classroom could hear his laughter.
當我告訴席德這個笑話時，他笑得很<u>大聲</u>。教室裡的每個人都可以聽見他的笑聲。

 (A) ***loudly*** 〔ˋlaʊdlɪ〕*adv.* 大聲地

 (B) secretly 〔ˋsikrɪtlɪ〕*adv.* 祕密地

 (C) strongly 〔ˋstrɔŋlɪ〕*adv.* 強烈地

 (D) weakly 〔ˋwiklɪ〕*adv.* 虛弱地

 * laugh 〔læf〕*v.* 笑 joke 〔dʒok〕*n.* 笑話
  laughter 〔ˋlæftə〕*n.* 笑聲

6. (**B**) Becky <u>orders</u> herself an orange juice in the café before her friends arrive.
貝琪在她的朋友到達之前，在咖啡廳為自己<u>點</u>了一杯柳橙汁。

 (A) change 〔tʃendʒ〕*v.* 改變 (B) ***order*** 〔ˋɔrdə〕*v.* 點餐

 (C) move 〔muv〕*v.* 移動 (D) wait 〔wet〕*v.* 等待

 * ***orange juice*** 柳橙汁 café 〔kəˋfe〕*n.* 咖啡廳

7. (**C**) Helen studies in a bilingual school. She <u>has been</u> there since she was 6 years old.

海倫在一所雙語學校唸書。她從六歲起就一直<u>在</u>那裡。

連接詞 since（自從）引導的副詞子句中，動詞時態用過去式，而主要子句的動詞時態則用「現在完成式」，表示「從過去持續到現在的動作或狀態」，故選 (C) *has been*。

* bilingual〔baɪˈlɪŋgwəl〕*adj.* 雙語的

8. (**C**) The weather in summer is not <u>only</u> hot but also wet. It's hard to imagine studying in a classroom without an air conditioner. 夏天天氣<u>不僅</u>炎熱，而且潮溼。很難想像在沒有冷氣機的教室唸書。

not only…but (also)~ 不僅…而且~

* weather〔ˈwɛðɚ〕*n.* 天氣　　wet〔wɛt〕*adj.* 潮溼的
  hard〔hɑrd〕*adj.* 困難的　　imagine〔ɪˈmædʒɪn〕*v.* 想像
  air conditioner 冷氣機

9. (**B**) The cafeteria was full, but Kevin saw an empty seat next to his classmate. "<u>May</u> I sit there?" Kevin asked his classmate. 自助餐廳擠滿了人，但凱文看到他同學旁邊有個空位。「我<u>可以</u>坐在那裡嗎？」凱文問他同學。

凱文是在徵求他同學的許可，故用助動詞 *May*「可以」。而 (A) Should「應該」，(C) Would 表「客氣的請求」，(D) Qill「將要」，皆不合句意。

* cafeteria〔ˌkæfəˈtɪrɪə〕*n.* 自助餐廳
  full〔fʊl〕*adj.* 客滿的　　empty〔ˈɛmptɪ〕*adj.* 空的
  seat〔sit〕*n.* 座位　　*next to* 在…旁邊

10. (**A**) Learning a second language <u>is</u> not as easy as you think.
學習第二外語不是像你想的那麼困難。

動名詞片語 Learning a second language 當主詞，視為
單數，後面須接單數動詞，故選 (A)。

* language〔'læŋgwɪdʒ〕*n.* 語言
second language （在母語以外所學的）第二語言

11. (**C**) Nick, no one can help you with this problem. You
should try to solve it by <u>yourself</u>.
尼克，沒有人可以幫你解決這個問題。你應該試著<u>自己</u>解決。

by oneself 獨力；靠自己

* **help** sb. **with** sth. 幫助某人某事
problem〔'prɑbləm〕*n.* 問題　　solve〔sɑlv〕*v.* 解決

12. (**B**) Paul will drive his car and Mandy will drive <u>hers</u>.
保羅將開他的車，曼蒂將開<u>她的車</u>。

…Mandy will drive *her car*.
= …Mandy will drive **hers**.

所有格代名詞用來代替「所有格＋名詞」，以避免重複
前面已提過的名詞。

13. (**A**) Please look before crossing the road and <u>walk</u> across
the street quickly.
請在穿越馬路之前看一看，並且快速<u>走</u>過街道。

本句為祈使句，省略主詞 you，而 and 為對等連接詞，前
後連接的兩個動詞，形式要一致，look 為原形動詞，故空
格須填一原形動詞，選 (A) **walk**。

* cross〔krɔs〕*v.* 橫越　　across〔ə'krɔs〕*prep.* 橫越

14. (**D**) Jessie has two sons; one works in the post office, and <u>the other</u> works in the hospital.

潔西有兩個兒子；一個在郵局工作，<u>另一個</u>在醫院工作。

  one…the other~ （兩者之中）一個…另一個~

  * ***post office*** 郵局　　hospital〔'hɑspɪtḷ〕*n.* 醫院

15. (**D**) Matt and Jen usually <u>go</u> to the library after school, but they didn't go there today.

麥特和貞通常在放學後<u>去</u>圖書館，但是今天他們沒有去。

  由頻率副詞 usually 可知，「下課後去圖書館」是習慣性的行為，故動詞要用「現在簡單式」，選 (D) ***go***。

  * library〔'laɪ,brɛrɪ〕*n.* 圖書館　　***after school*** 放學後

第二部份：段落填空

Questions 16-20

  Dogs have been man's good friend for thousands of years. There are many <u>stories</u> about brave dogs helping people in
  　　　　　　　　　　　　　　16
danger. <u>With</u> their help, many people lost in the mountains
　　　　　17
found their way home. Dogs can be stars, too. A dog called Lassie was the star of a popular <u>movie</u>.
　　　　　　　　　　　　　　　　18

  數千年以來，狗就一直是人類的好朋友。有很多關於勇敢的狗，幫助人們脫離險境的故事。很多在山上迷路的人，因為有狗的幫忙，才能順利找到回家的路。狗也可以當明星。有一隻叫萊西的狗，就曾經是一部賣座電影的明星。

man 〔 mæn 〕 n. 人類（集合名詞，表全體）

thousands of 數以千計的　　brave 〔 brev 〕 adj. 勇敢的

in danger 在危險中　　lost 〔 lɔst 〕 adj. 迷路的

in the mountains 在山中　　star 〔 stɑr 〕 n. 明星

call 〔 kɔl 〕 v. 稱爲；叫做　　popular 〔ˈpɑpjələ〕 adj. 受歡迎的

Dogs can hear and smell better than man, but they can't see
so well.　A dog lives about 12 or 13 years.　A thirteen-year-old
<u>　</u>19<u>　</u>　　　　　　　　　　　　　　　　　　　　　　　　20
child has not grown up yet, but a dog of that age is very old.

　　狗的聽覺跟嗅覺都比人類好，但是視覺就沒那麼好了。一隻狗的壽
命大概有十二到十三年。一個十三歲的小孩還沒發育完全，但是一隻相
同年紀的狗可就非常老了。

smell 〔 smɛl 〕 v. 聞；能分辨氣味　　***grow up*** 長大

not…yet 尚未　　age 〔 edʒ 〕 n. 年紀

16. (**A**)　(A) ***story*** 〔ˈstorɪ〕 n. 故事

　　　　　　(B) zoo 〔 zu 〕 n. 動物園

　　　　　　(C) picture 〔ˈpɪktʃə〕 n. 圖畫；照片

　　　　　　(D) opportunity 〔ˌɑpəˈtjunətɪ〕 n. 機會

17. (**C**)　介系詞 ***With*** 表「有」。

18. (**B**)　(A) store 〔 stor 〕 n. 商店

　　　　　　(B) ***movie*** 〔ˈmuvɪ〕 n. 電影

　　　　　　(C) restaurant 〔ˈrɛstərənt〕 n. 餐廳

　　　　　　(D) computer 〔 kəmˈpjutə〕 n. 電腦

19. (**C**) 依句意，相較之下，狗的視力沒那麼「好」，須用副詞 *well* 來修飾動詞 see，選 (C)。而 (A) 須改爲 clearly「清楚地」。

20. (**C**) 表示「…歲的」的複合形容詞中，單位名詞須用單數。

$$\begin{cases} \text{a thirteen-}\textit{year}\text{-old child （一個十三歲的孩子）} \\ = \text{a child who is thirteen } \textbf{years } \text{old} \end{cases}$$

Questions 21-25

Scott and I agreed to meet <u>at</u> 8:00 this morning, but he didn't
                                       21

show up until 9:00. "I've been waiting here for an hour," I said.

"This is the third <u>appointment</u> you've been late for this month."
                           22

Then I asked him if he was sorry, but he shook his head. "So I

was late," he said. "So what?" Then he walked away. Since

then, I <u>have been</u> very upset. In fact, I'm not sure I can be
       23

Scott's friend anymore. I <u>think</u> I'll go over to his house and <u>tell</u>
          24   25

him that now.

史卡特和我同意在今天早上八點鐘見面，可是他直到九點才出現。「我已經在這裡等了一個小時，」我說。「這是你這個月第三次約會遲到了。」然後我問他是不是覺得很抱歉，但他卻搖搖頭。「我就是遲到了，」他說。「那又怎麼樣？」然後就走開了。從那時候起，我就非常地不高興。事實上，我已經不知道要不要再把史考特當朋友看了。我想我要去他家，現在就跟他說清楚。

agree〔ə'gri〕v. 同意　　***show up*** 出現
until〔ən'tɪl〕*prep.* 直到　　***not…until~*** 直到～才…
late〔let〕*adj.* 遲到的　　if〔ɪf〕*conj.* 是否
sorry〔'sɔrɪ〕*adj.* 抱歉的
shake〔ʃek〕v. 搖（三態變化為：shake-shook-shaken）
shake one's head 搖頭（表示不同意）
So what? 那又怎麼樣？　　since〔sɪns〕*prep.* 自從
upset〔ʌp'sɛt〕*adj.* 不高興的　　***in fact*** 事實上
not…anymore 不再　　***go over to*** 前往

21. (**A**) 「在」八點鐘，介系詞用 ***at***。

22. (**B**) (A) chance〔tʃæns〕*n.* 機會
　　　　　(B) ***appointment***〔ə'pɔɪntmənt〕*n.* 約會
　　　　　(C) question〔'kwɛstʃən〕*n.* 問題
　　　　　(D) review〔rɪ'vju〕*n.* 複習；評論

23. (**B**) 從 since「自從」可知，動詞時態須用「現在完成式」，表示
　　　　　「從過去持續到現在的動作或狀態」，又主詞是 I，故選 (B)
　　　　　have been。

24. (**C**) 由 now 可知，須用「現在式」，且主詞是 I，故選 (C)
　　　　　think。

25. (**D**) and 為對等連接詞，go 為原形動詞，故空格也應填原形動
　　　　　詞，選 (D) ***tell***。

第三部份：閱讀理解

Questions 26-27

什麼活動：“P” 派對

為什麼　：慶祝瑞秋搬新家

什麼時候：八月九日，星期五晚上，九點鐘

什麼地方：瑞秋的新家

怎麼玩　：扮演 P 字母開頭的角色

celebrate〔'sɛlə,bret〕v. 慶祝　　move〔muv〕v. 搬家
role〔rol〕n. 角色　　**start with** 以～開始
letter〔'lɛtə〕n. 字母

26. (**B**) 派對 ＿＿＿＿＿＿＿。

　　(A) 將在星期五晚上舉行　　　(B) 將在瑞秋的新家舉行

　　(C) 是為了瑞秋的生日而舉辦　(D) 將在九月舉行

　　* hold〔hold〕v. 舉行

27. (**C**) 何者為真？

　　(A) 瑞秋要舉辦派對，是為了向她的朋友道別。

　　(B) 你可以裝扮成「老師」或「烏龜」。

　　(C) 你可以裝扮成「披薩外送員」或「馬鈴薯」。

　　(D) 任何參加派對的人必須自己帶食物。

　　* dress〔drɛs〕v. 裝扮　　as〔æz〕prep. 像是
　　turtle〔'tɝtḷ〕n. 烏龜　　pizza〔'pitsə〕n. 披薩
　　deliveryman〔dɪ'lɪvərɪmən〕n. 送貨員
　　potato〔pə'teto〕n. 馬鈴薯

Questions 28-29

早安！

這是凱莉老師在伯靈頓小學的英文一課程。

今天是九月九日，星期三。

課堂規定

1. 準時上課。
2. 舉手回答問題。
3. 專心聽老師講課。
4. 要做功課。

Ms.〔mɪz〕n. 女士　　*elementary school* 小學
rule〔rul〕n. 規定　　*on time* 準時
raise〔rez〕v. 舉起　　*pay attention to* 注意
homework〔'hom,wɝk〕n. 功課；家庭作業

28. (**A**) 老師是誰？

(A) 凱莉女士。　　　　　(B) 凱莉先生。
(C) 史都華女士。　　　　(D) 史都華先生。

29. (**C**) 這位英文老師不希望她的學生

(A) 舉手回答問題。　　　(B) 穿便服上課。
(C) 上課遲到。　　　　　(D) 做自己的作業。

* casual〔'kæʒuəl〕adj.（服裝）隨便的；非正式的
in class 在課堂上　　assignment〔ə'saɪnmənt〕n. 作業

Questions 30-32

Dear Ann,

My problem is my father is never home. He is a sales representative, and he is always going to the airport, or the train station, or the bus station. He is working in Kaohsiung this week. Next week he is going to Hualien. When my father *is* at home, he is tired, or he is working in his office. What can I do?

<u>Lonely</u> Son in Taipei

親愛的安：

我的問題是我爸爸從來不在家。他是業務代表，而且總是要去機場，或是火車站，或是客運車站。他這星期在高雄工作。下星期要去花蓮。當他*真的*在家的時候，不是很累，就是在辦公室工作。我要怎麼辦呢？

台北一個<u>孤單</u>的兒子

sales〔selz〕*adj.* 銷售的
representative〔ˌrɛprɪˈzɛntətɪv〕*n.* 代表
sales representative 業務代表　　airport〔ˈɛrˌport〕*n.* 機場
tired〔taɪrd〕*adj.* 疲累的　　office〔ˈɔfɪs〕*n.* 辦公室
lonely〔ˈlonlɪ〕*adj.* 孤單的　　son〔sʌn〕*n.* 兒子

30. (**D**) 小男孩的問題是什麼？

(A) 他爸爸失業。

(B) 他爸爸媽媽彼此不相愛。

(C) 他爸爸害怕搭飛機。

(D) 他爸爸努力工作，很少花時間跟他相處。

* lose〔luz〕v. 失去   job〔dʒab〕n. 工作
  each other 彼此   *be afraid to* + V. 害怕
  plane〔plen〕n. 飛機

31. (**C**) 他爸爸下星期要做什麼？

(A) 他要去美國出差。

(B) 他要和他的小孩去花蓮渡假。

(C) 他要去花蓮販售公司的商品。

(D) 他要待在台北，一整個禮拜都和家人在一起。

* *on business* 因為公事；出差
  holiday〔'halə,de〕n. 假期   goods〔gʊdz〕n. pl. 商品
  company〔'kʌmpənɪ〕n. 公司   stay〔ste〕v. 停留
  whole〔hol〕adj. 整個的

32. (**A**) 第九行裡的 "lonely" 意思是 _____ 。

(A) 不快樂的   (B) 興奮的

(C) 外向的   (D) 飢餓的

* line〔laɪn〕n. 行   excited〔ɪk'saɪtɪd〕adj. 興奮的
  outgoing〔'aʊt,goɪŋ〕adj. 外向的

Questions 33-35

Children and grownups enjoy playing with kites. There are a lot of kite festivals and competitions in China and many other countries. But kites are not just playthings. They can be useful in many other ways.

大人和小孩都喜歡玩風箏。在中國跟許多其他國家,都有很多關於風箏的節日跟競賽。但是風箏可不只是玩具。它們在其他許多方面也很有用處。

grownup〔'gron,ʌp〕n. 成人   ***play with*** 把玩
kite〔kaɪt〕n. 風箏   festival〔'fɛstəvl̩〕n. 節慶
competition〔,kɑmpə'tɪʃən〕n. 比賽
country〔'kʌntrɪ〕n. 國家   plaything〔'ple,θɪŋ〕n. 玩具
useful〔'jusfəl〕adj. 有用的   way〔we〕n. 方面

Kite flying has been popular in China for more than two thousand years. Scientists have been interested in kites for a long time. They have used them for studying the weather and for testing new kinds of flying machines. Today scientists have created many new kinds of kites. Some of these can pull boats or lift a man easily.

兩千多年來,放風箏在中國都一直很受歡迎。科學家長久以來都對風箏很有興趣。他們利用風箏研究氣候及測試新型的飛行器。現今科學家已經發明了很多新型的風箏。有些可以拉船,或者將一個人輕易地舉起來。

fly〔flaɪ〕v. 放(風箏)   China〔'tʃaɪnə〕n. 中國
more than 超過(= *over*)   scientist〔'saɪəntɪst〕n. 科學家
be interested in 對~有興趣   study〔'stʌdɪ〕v. 研究
test〔tɛst〕v. 測試   ***flying machine*** 飛行器
create〔krɪ'et〕v. 創造   pull〔pʊl〕v. 拉   boat〔bot〕n. 船
lift〔lɪft〕v. 舉起   easily〔'izɪlɪ〕adv. 輕易地

Some kites are really beautiful works of art. People are interested in kites because kite flying is both an art and a science. Most important of all, it is fun.

有些風箏眞的是美麗的藝術品。人們對風箏有興趣,是因爲放風箏,不只是種藝術,也是科學。最重要的是,放風箏很好玩。

work〔wɜk〕n. 作品　　art〔ɑrt〕n. 藝術
science〔'saɪəns〕n. 科學
most important of all 最重要的是　　fun〔fʌn〕adj. 好玩的

33. (**D**) ＿＿＿＿＿＿ 喜歡風箏。

(A) 小孩　　　　　　　　(B) 大人
(C) 只有中國的小孩跟大人　(D) 許多國家各種不同年齡的人

* adult〔ə'dʌlt〕n. 成人　　***of all ages*** 各種不同年齡的

34. (**B**) 人們沒有使用風箏來 ＿＿＿＿＿＿。

(A) 得知天氣的變化　　　　(B) 當作旅遊各國的方式
(C) 研究新機器　　　　　　(D) 當作空閒時好玩的活動

* change〔tʃendʒ〕n. 改變　　travel〔'trævl〕v. 旅行
from country to country 到各個國家
activity〔æk'tɪvətɪ〕n. 活動　　***free time*** 空閒時間

35. (**B**) 人們對風箏感興趣是因爲 ＿＿＿＿＿＿。

(A) 風箏很貴　　　　　　　(B) 風箏在科學方面很有用
(C) 放風箏是不錯的運動　　(D) 風箏是中國人發明的

* expensive〔ɪk'spɛnsɪv〕adj. 昂貴的
exercise〔'ɛksə‚saɪz〕n. 運動　　invent〔ɪn'vɛnt〕v. 發明
the Chinese 中國人

三、寫作能力測驗

第一部份：單句寫作

第 1～5 題：句子改寫

1. Jerry ：Did you bring the comic book?
   Carrie ：Oh, I forgot.
   Carrie forgot _____ comic book.

   重點結構：「forget + to V.」的用法

   解　答：Carrie forgot to bring the comic book.

   句型分析：主詞 + forget + to V.

   説　明：「忘記去做某件事」用 forget + to V. 來表示，此題須在 forgot（forget 的過去式）後面接不定詞。

   * *comic book* 漫畫書

2. My backpack is different from yours. （用 the same as）

   _____.

   重點結構：「the same as」的用法

   解　答：My backpack is not the same as yours.

   句型分析：主詞 + be 動詞 + the same as + 所有格代名詞

   説　明：以 not the same as「和～不一樣」取代 different from。

   * backpack〔'bæk‚pæk〕*n.* 背包
     different〔'dɪfrənt〕*adj.* 不同的
     be different from 和～不同
     same〔sem〕*adj.* 相同的
     be the same as 和～相同

3. When is the next movie?

   Tell us when _____.

   > 重點結構：間接問句做名詞子句

   > 解　答：<u>Tell us when the next movie is.</u>

   > 句型分析：Tell us + when + 主詞 + 動詞

   > 説　明：在 wh-問句前加 Tell us，形成間接問句，必須把
   > be 動詞 is 放在最後面，並把問號改成句點。

4. To keep a pet is not easy.

   It _____.

   > 重點結構：以 It 為虛主詞引導的句子

   > 解　答：<u>It is not easy to keep a pet.</u>

   > 句型分析：It is + 形容詞 + to V.

   > 説　明：虛主詞 It 代替不定詞片語，真正的主詞是不定詞
   > 片語 to keep a pet，則置於句尾。

   > * pet〔pɛt〕*n.* 寵物　　***keep a pet*** 養寵物

5. Mandy went to the gift shop.

   Why _____ the gift shop?

   > 重點結構：過去式的 wh-問句

   > 解　答：<u>Why did Mandy go to the gift shop?</u>

   > 句型分析：Why + did + 主詞 + 原形動詞？

   > 説　明：這一題應將過去式直述句改為 wh-問句，除了要加
   > 助動詞 did，還要記得助動詞後面的動詞，須用原形
   > 動詞，因此 went 要改成 go。

   > * ***gift shop*** 禮品店

第 6～10 題：句子合併

6. Patricia told Joyce something.

   John went home late.

   Patricia told Joyce why _____.

   > **重點結構**：名詞子句當受詞用
   >
   > **解　答**：Patricia told Joyce why John went home late.
   >
   > **句型分析**：Patricia told Joyce + why + 主詞 + 動詞
   >
   > **説　明**：Patricia 要告訴 Joyce 一件事，就是關於 John 晚
   > 回家這件事，兩句之間用疑問詞 why 來合併，如果
   > 是直接問句的話，我們會說："Why did John go
   > home late?"，但這裡前面有 Patricia told Joyce，
   > 因此後面必須接名詞子句，做為 Patricia told
   > Joyce 的受詞，即「疑問詞 + 主詞 + 動詞」的形
   > 式，在 Patricia told Joyce 後面接 why John went
   > home late。

7. I have a dog.

   My dog is sleeping right now.（用 that）

   I have a dog that _____.

   > **重點結構**：由 that 引導的形容詞了句
   >
   > **解　答**：I have a dog that is sleeping right now.
   >
   > **句型分析**：I have a dog + that + 動詞
   >
   > **説　明**：句意是「我有一隻狗，現在牠正在睡覺」，在合併
   > 兩句時，用 that 代替先行詞 a dog，引導形容詞子
   > 句，在子句中做主詞。

   * *right now* 現在（= now）

8. We moved the piano.

   My neighbors helped us.

   My neighbors helped us _____.

   重點結構：「help + *sb.* + (to) V.」的用法

   解　答：<u>My neighbors helped us (to) move the piano.</u>

   句型分析：help + 受詞 + 原形動詞或不定詞

   說　明：句意是「我的鄰居幫我們搬鋼琴」，用動詞 help 造
   　　　　句，help 之後所接的不定詞的 to 可省略。

   * neighbor〔'nebɚ〕*n.* 鄰居
   move〔muv〕*v.* 搬動

9. I went to the Museum of Fine Arts.

   I took the bus there.（用 by）

   I went _____ by _____.

   重點結構：「by + 交通工具」的用法

   解　答：<u>I went to the Museum of Fine Arts by bus.</u>

   句型分析：主詞 + 動詞 + by + 名詞

   說　明：這題的意思是說「我搭公車去美術館」，用「by +
   　　　　交通工具」，表「搭乘～（交通工具）」，注意交通
   　　　　工具不能加定冠詞 the。

   * museum〔mju'ziəm〕*n.* 博物館
   fine arts 美術

10. Linda is very old.

　　Linda cannot see well. (用 too…to)

　　Linda is too old _____.

　　　重點結構：「too + 形容詞 + to V.」的用法

　　　　解　答：<u>Linda is too old to see well.</u>

　　　句型分析：主詞 + be 動詞 + too + 形容詞 + to V.

　　　　說　明：這題的意思是說「琳達年紀太大，看不清楚」，用
　　　　　　　　 too…to V. 合併這兩句，表「太…以致於不～」。

第 11～15 題：重組

11. Would _____.

　　like / tea / cup / you / to have / a / of

　　　重點結構：「Would you like + to V.?」的用法

　　　　解　答：<u>Would you like to have a cup of tea?</u>

　　　句型分析：Would you like + 不定詞？

　　　　說　明：「Would you like～?」為徵詢某人是否要某物
　　　　　　　　 的用法，比「Do you want～?」更普遍，且更有
　　　　　　　　 禮貌。

12. Nancy _____.

　　most / questions / can / difficult / the / answer

　　　重點結構：形容詞最高級的用法

　　　　解　答：<u>Nancy can answer the most difficult questions.</u>

　　　句型分析：the most + 形容詞

　　　　說　明：difficult 為兩個音節以上的形容詞，故前面加
　　　　　　　　 most，形成最高級。

　　* difficult〔'dɪfə,kʌlt〕 adj. 困難的

13. The weather _____.

　　so / I / stay / that / is / hot / would rather / inside

　　　重點結構：「so + 形容詞 + that 子句」的用法

　　　解　答：The weather is so hot that I would rather stay inside.

　　　句型分析：主詞 + be 動詞 + so + 形容詞 + that + 主詞 + 動詞

　　　説　明：這題的意思是說「天氣太熱了，所以我寧願待在屋內」，合併兩句時，用「so…that～」，表「如此…以致於～」。

　　　＊ **would rather** + 原形 V. 寧願
　　　　inside〔ˋɪnˋsaɪd〕adv. 在室內

14. Paul _____.

　　has / sick / for / a / been / month

　　　重點結構：現在完成式字序

　　　解　答：Paul has been sick for a month.

　　　句型分析：主詞 + have/has + been + 形容詞 + for + 一段時間

　　　説　明：一般現在完成式的結構是「主詞 + have/has + 過去分詞」，be 動詞的現在完成式是 have/has been，而「for + 一段時間」，表「持續（多久）」，此時間片語置於句尾。

15. Kay _____.

afraid / taking / tests / is / of / English / not

重點結構：「be 動詞 + afraid + of + 動名詞」的用法

解　答：<u>Kay is not afraid of taking English tests.</u>

句型分析：主詞 + be 動詞 + afraid + of + 動名詞

說　明：afraid（害怕的）的用法為：

$$\begin{cases} \text{be 動詞 + afraid of + N / V-ing} \\ \text{be 動詞 + afraid + that + 主詞 + 動詞} \end{cases}$$

從 taking 可知，此題重組是第一種用法。

第二部份：段落寫作

題目：請根據圖片內容寫一篇約 50 字的簡短描述。

One morning my mother asked me to carry an umbrella to school. She said it would rain. **But** it was a sunny morning. I did not believe her, and I did not want to take an umbrella. I said "No!" loudly and went to school.

That afternoon it rained. The rain was heavy. I got wet because I did not have an umbrella. **That night** I began to cough and sneeze. I had caught a cold. **Next time** I will listen to my mother.

carry〔ˋkærɪ〕v. 攜帶　　umbrella〔ʌmˋbrɛlə〕n. 雨傘
rain〔ren〕v. 下雨　　sunny〔ˋsʌnɪ〕adj. 陽光普照的
believe〔bɪˋliv〕v. 相信　　loudly〔ˋlaʊdlɪ〕adv. 大聲地
heavy〔ˋhɛvɪ〕adj. 大量的　　wet〔wɛt〕adj. 濕的
cough〔kɔf〕v. 咳嗽　　sneeze〔sniz〕v. 打噴嚏
catch a cold 感冒　　***next time*** 下一次
listen to 聽從

全民英語能力分級檢定測驗
初級測驗②

一、聽力測驗

　　本測驗分三部份，全爲三選一之選擇題，每部份各 10 題，共 30 題，作答時間約 20 分鐘。

第一部份：看圖辨義

　　　　　本部份共 10 題，試題冊上每題有一個圖片，請聽錄音機
　　　　　播出一個相關的問題，與 A、B、C 三個英語敘述後，選
　　　　　一個與所看到圖片最相符的答案，並在答案紙上相對的圓
　　　　　圈內塗黑作答。每題播出一遍，問題及選項均不印在試題
　　　　　冊上。

例：（看）　　　　　　　　　　（聽）

NT$80　　NT$50

Look at the picture.　How
much is the hamburger?

A.　It's eighty dollars.
B.　It's fifty-five dollars.
C.　It's eighteen dollars.

正確答案爲 A

Question 1

Question 2

Question 3

Question 4

Question 5

Question 6

請翻頁 ▐▊⇨

Question 7

Question 8

Question 9

Question 10

請 翻 頁 ⫸

第二部份：問答

　　本部份共 10 題，每題錄音機會播出一個問句或直述句，每題播出一次，聽後請從試題冊上 A、B、C 三個選項中，選出一個最適合的回答或回應，並在答案紙上塗黑作答。

例：

（聽）　Good morning, Kevin. How are you?

（看）　A. I'm fine, thank you.
　　　　B. I'm in the living room.
　　　　C. My name is Kevin.

　　　　正確答案為 A

11. A. My family and I went to a movie last night.
　　B. I can't answer that.
　　C. Who were you calling?

12. A. I just watched TV.
　　B. I had a great time.
　　C. About nine.

13. A. Have a nice trip!
　　B. You should see a doctor.
　　C. Where is it?

14. A. We can take six comfortably.
　　B. Nine is too many.
　　C. It's a size four.

15. A. I began school at the
       age of seven.
    B. Ten minutes before
       the first class.
    C. I usually take a bus.

16. A. I'm giving him a
       new CD.
    B. Happy birthday,
       Steve!
    C. What do you want?

17. A. Yes, I am.
    B. No, I don't.
    C. Yes, I do.

18. A. It weighs one
       kilogram.
    B. It costs one hundred
       dollars.
    C. There are eight
       oranges in one kilo.

19. A. I don't like pizza
       very much.
    B. To go, please.
    C. I'm hungry.

20. A. You are, too.
    B. Don't mention it.
    C. You don't say!

請 翻 頁 ▮◳⟹

第三部份： 簡短對話

本部份共 10 題，每題錄音機會播出一段對話及一個相關的問題，每題播出兩次，聽後請從試題冊上 A、B、C 三個選項中，選出一個最適合的回答，並在答案紙上塗黑作答。

例：

（聽）(Woman)　Good afternoon, …Mr. Davis?

　　　(Man)　　Yes.　I have an appointment with Dr. Sanders at two o'clock.　My son Tommy has a fever.

　　　(Woman)　Oh, that's too bad.　Well, please have a seat, Mr. Davis.　Dr. Sanders will be right with you.

　　　Question: Where did this conversation take place?

（看）A.　In a post office.

　　　B.　In a restaurant.

　　　C.　In a doctor's office.

　　　正確答案爲 C

21. A. He thinks it isn't
    long enough.
  B. He thinks it is very
    interesting.
  C. He thinks it will take
    a long time to finish.

22. A. She is a flight attendant.
  B. She is a waitress.
  C. She is a driver.

23. A. He will buy the Harry
    Potter book for the
    girl.
  B. He will lend the book
    to the girl.
  C. The girl should finish
    the book before he
    does.

24. A. She was upset.
  B. Her mother was
    very happy.
  C. She got poor
    grades.

25. A. She has a red
    jacket.
  B. She is the girl's
    new friend.
  C. She is a new
    student.

26. A. She wants him to
    be quiet.
  B. She wants him to
    study.
  C. She wants him to
    close the window.

請 翻 頁 ⟥⟫⟹

27. A. Her brother will
       study abroad.
    B. She has not seen her
       brother for two years.
    C. Her brother is
       coming home.

28. A. Turn on the
       television.
    B. Go to the window.
    C. Open her eyes.

29. A. Because she doesn't
       want to miss the
       program.
    B. In a half hour.
    C. It is eleven o'clock.

30. A. She will tell Ann.
    B. She will tell the cake
       store.
    C. She will tell Ann's
       friends.

二、閱讀能力測驗

本測驗分三部份，全為四選一之選擇題，共 35 題，作答時間 35 分鐘。

第一部份： 詞彙和結構

本部份共 15 題，每題含一個空格。請就試題冊上 A、B、C、D 四個選項中選出最適合題意的字或詞，標示在答案紙上。

1. The old picture _____ me of my happy childhood in the countryside.
   A. reminded
   B. remembered
   C. recorded
   D. returned

2. Could we have the _____, please? We'd like to order now.
   A. mouse
   B. menu
   C. machine
   D. message

3. Don't watch that TV show. It would be a _____ of time.
   A. space
   B. while
   C. moment
   D. waste

請 翻 頁 ⟩⟩⟩⟫

4. Salesman : Would you like the blue skirt or the red one?

   Elizabeth : I have no idea. I can't _____ up my mind.

   A. make

   B. open

   C. build

   D. keep

5. Stop showing _____—we all know how clever you are!

   A. up

   B. in

   C. out

   D. off

6. You must be _____ when you're holding a little baby.

   A. strict

   B. gentle

   C. smart

   D. natural

7. I can't believe that Zoe is cooking today. She _____ does the cooking at home.

   A. always

   B. usually

   C. seldom

   D. finally

8. I met Susie when I was in the U.S. We always send
   _____ Christmas cards.
   A. each other
   B. another
   C. the other
   D. both

9. My parents don't let us _____ TV after 10 o'clock.
   A. watched
   B. to watch
   C. watching
   D. watch

10. Laura didn't have lunch until two o'clock this afternoon.
    Right now she _____ beef noodles.
    A. has
    B. has had
    C. was having
    D. is having

11. Eddie's handwriting is so poor _____ his teacher cannot
    accept his papers.
    A. than
    B. that
    C. as
    D. if

請 翻 頁 ⟹

12. _____ I came home, Little Spot ran to me and welcomed
    me home.
    A. Before
    B. By the way
    C. As soon as
    D. After all

13. I _____ live in Taipei, but now I live in Taichung.
    A. use to
    B. be used to
    C. was used to
    D. used to

14. Sarah was not _____ in fashion news at all.
    A. interesting
    B. interests
    C. interested
    D. interest

15. _____ you take enough rest, you will get better.
    A. Although
    B. As long as
    C. Even if
    D. That

第二部份：段落填空

本部份共 10 題，包括二個段落，每個段落各含 5 個空格。
請就試題冊上 A、B、C、D 四個選項中選出最適合題意
的字或詞，標示在答案紙上。

Questions 16-20

I ___(16)___ a nice junior high school in Taipei. My school
is very close to the sea, so in my biology class, we often
___(17)___ trips to the ___(18)___ to study the fish life. Students
and teachers from other places in Taiwan come to visit my
school very often, because it is a very special school. We are
good in many different ___(19)___, especially math and science.
We have won awards in many math competitions and science
exhibitions. I'm so proud ___(20)___ a student at my school.

16. A. arrive
    B. attend
    C. agree
    D. appear

17. A. take
    B. go with
    C. go
    D. walk

18. A. museum
    B. mountains
    C. sea
    D. sky

19. A. lessons
    B. subways
    C. games
    D. subjects

20. A. to be
    B. of be
    C. to being
    D. in being

請翻頁 ◁▯▭▭▭▷

Questions 21-25

No one can learn a language well ___(21)___ a good dictionary. It is an important tool and it will tell you ___(22)___ what a word means but also how it is used. As a language changes with time, a good dictionary needs ___(23)___ about every ten years. A good dictionary will tell you many interesting facts, like the pronunciation and meanings of a word. It will also tell you how a simple word can be used ___(24)___ different ways. So before you use a dictionary, ___(25)___ sure to read the front part to learn how to use it well.

21. A. by
    B. for
    C. with
    D. without

22. A. not only
    B. both
    C. only
    D. only not

23. A. change
    B. changed
    C. to changing
    D. to be changed

24. A. to
    B. by
    C. in
    D. on

25. A. to be
    B. being
    C. be
    D. it is

第三部份： 閱讀理解

本部份共 10 題，包括數段短文，每段短文後有 1～3 個相
關問題，請就試題冊上 A、B、C、D 四個選項中選出最
適合者，標示在答案紙上。

Questions 26-27

26. What does this sign mean?
    A. You have to watch for children.
    B. You have to cross the street.
    C. You can drive quickly.
    D. You cannot walk alone.

27. Where will you most likely see this sign?
    A. Near a zoo.
    B. Near a school.
    C. Near an airport.
    D. Near a parking lot.

請 翻 頁 ▐▌⟹

Questions 28-30

The following chart shows the different percentage of basketball fans and badminton fans in different age groups. Study the line graph carefully and answer the questions.

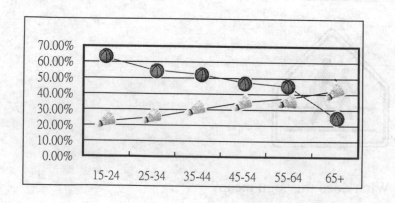

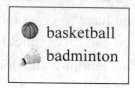

🏀 basketball

badminton

28. Among which age group does basketball have its greatest number of fans?
    A. 15-24.
    B. 35-44.
    C. 55-64.
    D. 65+.

29. The graph shows that badminton is most popular in the
    _____ age group.
    A. 15-24.
    B. 35-44.
    C. 55-64.
    D. 65+.

30. Which of the following is true?
    A. People of all ages like basketball more than badminton.
    B. Among 15 to 24 year olds, the difference between the
       percentage of basketball fans and the percentage of
       badminton fans is 40 points.
    C. Old people don't play basketball and badminton.
    D. Badminton is as popular as basketball for people from
       age 35 to age 44.

請 翻 頁 ⅢⅢ⟹

Questions 31-32

From: peter7788@hotmail.com

To: bbecky@aol.com

Subject: My homepage is coming soon!

Dear Rebecca,

How's everything with you now? Well, I'm now working on my homepage on the Web. I plan to open it on September 1st, and the address of this wonderful site is http://www.gept.idv.tw. You know, a lot of information about music and movies, which are my hobbies, will be available. I also hope to make many links. Why don't you pop in to my page? I can't wait to know your opinions.

Have a nice day!

Peter

31. What is true of Peter's homepage?

A. The homepage is about his school life.

B. The homepage has been open for four months.

C. The homepage is scheduled to open in September.

D. The homepage has information on learning English.

32. The phrase "pop in" in the e-mail means _____.

A. visit

B. make a sound

C. jump

D. preview

請 翻 頁 ◫⟹

Questions 33-35

Do you know the story about where the word "hamburger" came from? Almost a hundred years ago, some Germans came to the United States. One day when they were cooking some round pieces of beef, some Americans saw them and asked them what they were making. Because those Germans did not understand the question, they thought the Americans were asking them where they came from. They answered, "Hamburg."

One of the Americans was a restaurant owner. He knew that many Americans loved to eat sandwiches, so he put the round pieces of cooked beef in buns. He called his sandwiches hamburgers. Today, hamburgers are still very popular in fast-food restaurants and people around the world know what hamburgers are.

33. Who made a hamburger first?
   A. Mr. Hamburg.
   B. An American in Hamburg.
   C. Mr. Germans.
   D. An American who owned a restaurant.

34. From the passage we know that the hamburger in early times does NOT have _____.
    A. bread
    B. beef
    C. ham
    D. buns

35. Which of the following is true?
    A. Hamburg is the name of a city in the United States.
    B. Germans knew that Americans loved beef.
    C. Not many people like to order hamburgers at fast-food restaurants.
    D. The Germans did not clearly understand the meaning of the question asked by the Americans.

請 翻 頁 ⨀⟹

三、寫作能力測驗

　　本測驗共有兩部份,第一部份為單句寫作,第二部份為段落寫作。測驗時間為 40 分鐘。

第一部份: 單句寫作

　　　　　　請將答案寫在寫作能力測驗答案紙對應的題號旁,如有拼字、標點、大小寫之錯誤,將予扣分。

第 1~5 題: 句子改寫

　　　　　　請依題目之提示,將原句改寫成指定型式,並將改寫的句子完整地寫在答案紙上(包括提示之文字及標點符號)。

1. Paula asked me, "Could you lend me your umbrella?"

   Paula asked me if _____ lend her my umbrella.

2. Frank is taller than all the other students in his class.

   Frank _____ tallest _____ in his class.

3. Andy overslept, so he was late for school.

   Andy _____ because _____.

4. Matt will go to junior high school.

   When _____?

5. Nancy watches cartoons every night.

   Nancy _____ last night.

第6～10題：句子合併

請依照題目指示，將兩句合併成一句，並將合併的句子
完整地寫在答案紙上（包括提示之文字及標點符號）。

6. May likes to listen to music.
   May also likes to go climbing.

   May likes to _____.

7. How much does it cost?
   I don't know.

   I don't know how _____.

8. Tim has cats.
   Eva is Tim's cat.

   Eva _____ one of _____.

9. Fred is 155cm tall.
   Robert is 155cm tall, too.

   Fred _____ as Robert.

10. Judy goes jogging.
    Then, she has breakfast.

    Judy _____ before _____.

請翻頁

第 11~15 題：重組

　　　　請將題目中所有提示字詞整合成一有意義的句子，並
　　　　將重組的句子完整地寫在答案紙上（包括提示之文字
　　　　及標點符號）。答案中必須使用所有提示字詞，且不
　　　　能隨意增加字詞，否則不予計分。

11. Kelly _____.

　　 been learning / has / for / karate / seven years

12. He _____.

　　 to make / with / my brother / wants / friends

13. Iris bought _____.

　　 at the bookstore / this pencil box / the park / next to

14. How many _____?

　　 in the basket / are / eggs / there

15. The _____.

　　 and / sweet / tastes / sour / soup

第二部份：段落寫作

題目：爸爸買了一輛新腳踏車給我，並且教我如何騎腳踏車。經過
不斷的嚐試，我終於學會了。請根據圖片內容寫一篇約50字
的簡短描述。

初級英檢模擬試題②詳解

一、聽力測驗

第一部份

Look at the picture for question 1.

1. (**B**) What is he?

      A. He is a mechanic.

      B. He is a truck driver.

      C. He is a driving teacher.

      * ***What is*** *sb.?* 某人的職業是什麼？

       (= *What does sb. do?*)

      mechanic〔məˋkænɪk〕*n.* 技工

      truck〔trʌk〕*n.* 卡車

      driver〔ˋdraɪvɚ〕*n.* 司機

      driving teacher 汽車教練

Look at the picture for question 2.

2. (**A**) What does he like to do?

      A. He likes to swim underwater.

      B. He likes to go surfing.

      C. He likes to go fishing.

      * swim〔swɪm〕*v.* 游泳

      underwater〔ˋʌndɚ͵wɔtɚ〕*adv.* 在水中

      go surfing 去衝浪   ***go fishing*** 去釣魚

Look at the picture for question 3.

3. (**B**) How many children are on each basketball team?

        A. Eight.

        B. Four.

        C. One.

       * each〔 itʃ 〕*adj.* 每個

         basketball〔'bæskɪtˌbɔl 〕*n.* 籃球

         team〔 tim 〕*n.* 隊

Look at the picture for question 4.

4. (**C**) What is she doing in the kitchen?

        A. She is baking.

        B. She is doing the dishes.

        C. She is cooking.

       * bake〔 bek 〕*v.* 烘烤（麵包、蛋糕等）

        do the dishes 洗碗   cook〔 kʊk 〕*v.* 煮飯

Look at the picture for question 5.

5. (**C**) Which is true?

        A. Rebecca is happier than Wendy.

        B. Wendy is shorter than Rebecca.

        C. Wendy is more fashionable than Rebecca.

       * true〔 tru 〕*adj.* 眞實的；正確的   short〔 ʃɔrt 〕*adj.* 矮的

        fashionable〔'fæʃənəbḷ 〕*adj.* 時髦的

Look at the picture for question 6.

6. (**B**) What do the children have?

　　　　A. They are all having a good time.

　　　　B. They all have lanterns.

　　　　C. They all have dolls.

　　　　* ***have a good time*** 玩得愉快

　　　　　lantern〔ˈlæntən〕*n.* 燈籠

　　　　　doll〔dɑl〕*n.* 玩偶；洋娃娃

Look at the picture for question 7.

7. (**B**) Which dress has buttons?

　　　　A. The right one.

　　　　B. The less expensive one.

　　　　C. The one with the hat.

　　　　* dress〔drɛs〕*n.* 洋裝　　button〔ˈbʌtn̩〕*n.* 鈕扣

　　　　　right〔raɪt〕*adj.* 右邊的

　　　　　expensive〔ɪkˈspɛnsɪv〕*adj.* 昂貴的

　　　　　hat〔hæt〕*n.* 帽子

Look at the picture for question 8.

8. (**A**) What is he doing?

　　　　A. He is taking a bath.

　　　　B. He is taking a shower.

　　　　C. He is taking a nap.

　　　　* ***take a bath*** 泡澡　　***take a shower*** 淋浴

　　　　　take a nap 小睡片刻

Look at the picture for question 9.

9. (**C**) What must he do?

    A. He must finish his lunch.

    B. He must eat the candy.

    C. He must take medicine.

    * must〔mʌst〕*aux.* 必須　　finish〔'fɪnɪʃ〕*v.* 吃完
    candy〔'kændɪ〕*n.* 糖果
    take medicine 吃藥

Look at the picture for question 10.

10. (**A**) Where did he write?

    A. He wrote on the blackboard.

    B. He is writing his homework.

    C. He wrote a math problem.

    * blackboard〔'blæk,bord〕*n.* 黑板
    homework〔'hom,wɝk〕*n.* 家庭作業
    math〔mæθ〕*n.* 數學　　problem〔'prɑbləm〕*n.* 問題

第二部份

11. (**A**) I called you last night, but no one answered.

    A. My family and I went to a movie last night.

    B. I can't answer that.

    C. Who were you calling?

    * call〔kɔl〕*v.* 打電話給～
    answer〔'ænsɚ〕*v.* 接電話；回答
    go to a movie 去看電影

12. (**C**) What time did you get home last night?

    A. I just watched TV.

    B. I had a great time.

    C. About nine.

    * ***have a great time*** 玩得很愉快 (= *have a good time*)

13. (**B**) I think I have the flu.

    A. Have a nice trip!

    B. You should see a doctor.

    C. Where is it?

    * flu 〔flu〕 *n.* 流行性感冒

    Have a nice trip! 祝你玩得愉快！

14. (**A**) How many people can fit in the car?

    A. We can take six comfortably.

    B. Nine is too many.

    C. It's a size four.

    * fit 〔fɪt〕 *v.* 被容納   take 〔tek〕 *v.* 容納

    comfortably 〔'kʌmfɚtəblɪ〕 *adv.* 充裕地

    size 〔saɪz〕 *n.* 尺寸

15. (**B**) What time do you usually get to school?

    A. I began school at the age of seven.

    B. Ten minutes before the first class.

    C. I usually take a bus.

    * ***get to*** 到達   ***begin school*** 開始上學 (= *start school*)

    at the age of 在～歲時

16. (**A**) What did you get Steve for his birthday?

      A. I'm giving him a new CD.

      B. Happy birthday, Steve!

      C. What do you want?

      * get〔gɛt〕*v.* 買 (= *buy*)

17. (**A**) Are you studying now?

      A. Yes, I am.

      B. No, I don't.

      C. Yes, I do.

18. (**B**) How much is a kilo of oranges?

      A. It weighs one kilogram.

      B. It costs one hundred dollars.

      C. There are eight oranges in one kilo.

      * *How much ~?* ~多少錢？
        kilo〔'kɪlo〕*n.* 公斤 (= kilogram〔'kɪlə,græm〕)
        orange〔'ɔrɪndʒ〕*n.* 柳橙　　weigh〔we〕*v.* 重~

19. (**C**) Why did you order such a large pizza?

      A. I don't like pizza very much.

      B. To go, please.

      C. I'm hungry.

      * order〔'ɔrdə〕*v.* 點餐　　large〔lardʒ〕*adj.* 大的
        pizza〔'pitsə〕*n.* 披薩　　*to go* 外帶 (↔ *for here* 內用)
        hungry〔'hʌŋgrɪ〕*adj.* 飢餓的

20. (**B**) Thank you for a wonderful meal.

　　　A. You are, too.

　　　B. Don't mention it.

　　　C. You don't say!

　　　* wonderful〔'wʌndəˌfəl〕adj. 極好的

　　　　meal〔mil〕n. 一餐

　　　　Don't mention it. 不客氣。(= *You're welcome.*)

　　　　You don't say! 你不是說眞的吧；眞沒想到！（表驚訝）

第三部份

21. (**C**) M : Have you finished the history assignment?

　　　W : No. It's very long, isn't it?

　　　M : Yes. I've already spent two hours on it and I'm nowhere near finished.

　　　Question : What does the boy think of the history assignment?

　　　A. He thinks it isn't long cnough.

　　　B. He thinks it is very interesting.

　　　C. He thinks it will take a long time to finish.

　　　* history〔'hɪstrɪ〕n. 歷史

　　　　assignment〔ə'saɪnmənt〕n. 作業

　　　　spend + 時間 + ***on*** + ***N.*** 花費時間做~

　　　　nowhere near 一點也不；差得遠 (= *not at all*)

　　　　finished〔'fɪnɪʃt〕adj. 完成的　　***think of*** 認爲

　　　　interesting〔'ɪntrɪstɪŋ〕adj. 有趣的

　　　　take〔tek〕v. 花費（時間）

22. (**A**) W：This way, sir. 21B is your seat.

M：Thank you. Could you bring me a Coke?

W：I'm sorry, sir. You'll have to wait until after we take off.

Question：Who is the woman?

A. She is a flight attendant.

B. She is a waitress.

C. She is a driver.

* ***This way, sir.*** 先生，請走這邊。　　seat〔sit〕*n.* 座位
Coke〔kok〕*n.* 可口可樂（= *Coca-cola*）
take off 起飛　　attendant〔ə'tɛndənt〕*n.* 服務員
flight attendant 空服員
waitress〔'wetrɪs〕*n.* 女服務生

23. (**B**) W：I see you're reading the new Harry Potter book.

M：Yes, and I'm really enjoying it.

W：I plan to read it, too. Maybe I'll buy it next week.

M：Oh, don't do that. You can read mine when I'm finished.

Question：What does the boy mean?

A. He will buy the Harry Potter book for the girl.

B. He will lend the book to the girl.

C. The girl should finish the book before he does.

* plan〔plæn〕*v.* 打算　　maybe〔'mebɪ〕*adv.* 可能
mean〔min〕*v.* 意思是　　lend〔lɛnd〕*v.* 借（出）

24. (**C**) M：You look upset.

W：I just had a quarrel with my mother.

M：What about?

W：She is not happy with my grades.

Question：Why did the girl quarrel with her mother?

A. She was upset.

B. She mother was very happy.

C. She got poor grades.

* upset〔ʌpˋsɛt〕*adj.* 心煩的；不高興的
quarrel〔ˋkwɔrəl〕*n. v.* 爭吵
What about? 吵什麼？(= *What did you quarrel about?*)
grade〔gred〕*n.* 分數；成績
poor〔pʊr〕*adj.* 差勁的

25. (**C**) W：Do you know what her name is?

M：Who?

W：The girl with the red jacket.

M：Oh, that's Emily. She's a new student here.

Question：Who is Emily?

A. She has a red jacket.

B. She is the girl's new friend.

C. She is a new student.

* jacket〔ˋdʒækɪt〕*n.* 夾克

26. (**C**) W : Please close the window.

M : All right. Are you too cold?

W : No, but the neighbors are noisy and I'm trying to study.

Question : What does the girl want the boy to do?

A. She wants him to be quiet.

B. She wants him to study.

C. She wants him to close the window.

* ***All right.*** 好的。　　neighbor〔'nebɚ〕*n.* 鄰居
noisy〔'nɔɪzɪ〕*adj.* 吵鬧的　　quiet〔'kwaɪət〕*adj.* 安靜的

27. (**C**) M : You seem very happy today.

W : I'm excited. My brother is coming home from England.

M : How long has he been there?

W : Two years.

M : Was he working there?

W : No. He was studying.

Question : What is the girl happy about?

A. Her brother will study abroad.

B. She has not seen her brother for two years.

C. Her brother is coming home.

* seem〔sim〕*v.* 似乎　　excited〔ɪk'saɪtɪd〕*adj.* 興奮的
England〔'ɪŋglənd〕*n.* 英國
abroad〔ə'brɔd〕*adv.* 到國外

28. (**B**) M : Have you looked outside?

        W : No. Why?

        M : It's snowing.

        W : Really? This is something I have to see.

        Question : What will the girl probably do next?

        A. Turn on the television.

        B. Go to the window.

        C. Open her eyes.

        * outside〔'aut'said〕adv. 向外面
          snow〔sno〕v. 下雪   probably〔'prɑbəblɪ〕adv. 大概
          next〔nɛkst〕adv. 接下來
          turn on 打開（電器）(↔ *turn off*)

29. (**B**) W : Could you tell me the time?

        M : Sure. It's 10:30. Why?

        W : There's a program on TV at 11:00 that I don't
            want to miss.

        Question : When will the girl watch television?

        A. Because she doesn't want to miss the program.

        B. In a half hour.

        C. It is eleven o'clock.

        * sure〔ʃur〕adv. 當然
          program〔'progræm〕n. 節目
          miss〔mɪs〕v. 錯過
          in a half hour 再過半個小時 (= *in half an hour*)

30. (**C**) W：What should we do for Ann's birthday?

M：Why don't we give her a surprise party?

W：Good idea. You get a cake and I'll tell everyone else.

Question：Who will the girl tell about the party?

A. She will tell Ann.

B. She will tell the cake store.

C. She will tell Ann's friends.

* surprise〔sə'praɪz〕*n.* 驚喜
  give sb. a party 為某人舉行派對　　get〔gɛt〕*v.* 買
  cake〔kek〕*n.* 蛋糕　　***tell about*** 講述

二、閱讀能力測驗

第一部份：詞彙和結構

1. (**A**) The old picture <u>reminded</u> me of my happy childhood in the countryside.

這張舊照片使我回想起在鄉下渡過的快樂童年。

(A) ***remind***〔rɪ'maɪnd〕*v.* 使想起
   remind sb. of sth. 使某人想起某事

(B) remember〔rɪ'mɛmbɚ〕*v.* 記得

(C) record〔rɪ'kɔrd〕*v.* 記錄

(D) return〔rɪ'tɝn〕*v.* 歸還

* picture〔'pɪktʃɚ〕*n.* 照片
  childhood〔'tʃaɪld͵hʊd〕*n.* 童年
  countryside〔'kʌntrɪ͵saɪd〕*n.* 鄉下

2. (**B**) Could we have the <u>menu</u>, please? We'd like to order
now. 請給我們<u>菜單</u>，好嗎？我們現在想要點餐。

    (A) mouse〔maʊs〕*n.* 老鼠；滑鼠

    (B) ***menu***〔'mɛnju〕*n.* 菜單

    (C) machine〔mə'ʃin〕*n.* 機器

    (D) message〔'mɛsɪdʒ〕*n.* 訊息

    * ***would like to*** + *V.* 想要   order〔'ɔrdə〕*v.* 點餐

3. (**D**) Don't watch that TV show. It would be a <u>waste</u> of time.
別看那個電視節目。那會<u>浪費</u>時間。

    (A) space〔spes〕*n.* 空間

    (B) while〔hwaɪl〕*n.* 一會兒

    (C) moment〔'moмənt〕*n.* 片刻

    (D) ***waste***〔west〕*n.* 浪費

    * show〔ʃo〕*n.* 節目

4. (**A**) Salesman : Would you like the blue skirt or the red one?
Elizabeth : I have no idea. I can't <u>make</u> up my mind.
售 貨 員：妳想要藍色的裙子，或是紅色的？
伊莉莎白：我不知道。我無法<u>決</u>定。

    make up one's ***mind*** 下定決心

    * salesman〔'selzmən〕*n.* 售貨員   skirt〔skɝt〕*n.* 裙子
    I have no idea. 我不知道。(= *I don't know.*)

5. (**D**) Stop showing <u>off</u>—we all know how clever you are!
別再<u>炫耀</u>了——我們都知道你有多聰明！

    show off 炫耀

    * ***stop*** + *V-ing* 停止做~   clever〔'klɛvə〕*adj.* 聰明的

6. (**B**) You must be <u>gentle</u> when you're holding a little baby.

當你在抱小嬰兒時，必須要<u>溫柔</u>。

(A) strict〔strɪkt〕*adj.* 嚴格的

(B) ***gentle***〔'dʒɛntl̩〕*adj.* 溫柔的

(C) smart〔smɑrt〕*adj.* 聰明的

(D) natural〔'nætʃərəl〕*adj.* 自然的

* hold〔hold〕*v.* 抱著　　baby〔'bebɪ〕*n.* 嬰兒

7. (**C**) I can't believe that Zoe is cooking today. She <u>seldom</u> does the cooking at home.

我不敢相信柔伊今天要煮飯。她<u>很少</u>在家裡做飯。

按照句意，柔伊煮飯是出乎意料之外的事情，故選 (C) ***seldom***「很少」，表示她做飯的頻率很低。而 (A) always 「總是」，(B) usually「通常」，(D) finally「最後」， 均不合句意。

* believe〔bɪ'liv〕*v.* 相信
  cook〔kʊk〕*v.* 煮飯 (= *do the cooking*)

8. (**A**) I met Susie when I was in the U.S. We always send <u>each other</u> Christmas cards.

我在美國認識蘇西。我們總是<u>互相</u>寄聖誕卡。

each other 互相

(B) another「(三者以上) 另一個」，(C) the other「(兩 者中) 另一個」，(D) both「兩者都」，均不合句意。

* meet〔mit〕*v.* 認識　　send〔sɛnd〕*v.* 寄
  Christmas〔'krɪsməs〕*n.* 聖誕節　　card〔kɑrd〕*n.* 卡片

9. (**D**) My parents don't let us <u>watch</u> TV after 10 o'clock.

我父母不讓我們在十點鐘以後看電視。

let 為使役動詞，接受詞後，須接原形動詞。

10. (**D**) Laura didn't have lunch until two o'clock this afternoon. Right now she <u>is having</u> beef noodles.

蘿拉今天直到下午兩點鐘才吃午餐。現在她<u>正在吃牛肉麵</u>。

從時間副詞 right now 可知，吃牛肉麵是正在進行的動作，故動詞時態用「現在進行式」。

* until〔ən'tɪl〕*prep.* 直到　　***not…until~*** 直到~才…
right now 現在　　have〔hæv〕*v.* 吃
beef noodles 牛肉麵

11. (**B**) Eddie's handwriting is so poor <u>that</u> his teacher cannot accept his papers.

艾迪的字跡太潦草了，<u>所以</u>他的老師無法接受他的報告。

so…that~ 如此…以致於~

* handwriting〔'hænd,raɪtɪŋ〕*n.* 筆跡
poor〔pur〕*adj.* 差勁的　　accept〔ək'sɛpt〕*v.* 接受
paper〔'pepɚ〕*n.* 報告

12. (**C**) <u>As soon as</u> I came home, Little Spot ran to me and welcomed me home.

我<u>一</u>回到家，小花<u>就</u>跑向我，歡迎我回家。

as soon as 一…就~（連接詞片語）

而 (A) before「在~之前」，(B) by the way「順便一提」，(D) after all「畢竟」，句意及文法均不合。

* spot〔spɑt〕*n.* 斑點　　welcome〔'wɛlkəm〕*v.* 歡迎

13. (**D**) I <u>used to</u> live in Taipei, but now I live in Taichung.

我<u>以前</u>住在台北，但是現在我住在台中。

used to + 原形 *V.* 以前

而 (B)(C) be 動詞 + used to + V-ing 表「習慣於」，
則用法不合。

14. (**C**) Sarah was not <u>interested</u> in fashion news at all.

莎拉對流行資訊一點都不<u>感興趣</u>。

(A) interesting〔ˈɪntrɪstɪŋ〕*adj.* 有趣的

(B) interest〔ˈɪntrɪst〕*v.* 使感興趣

(C) **interested**〔ˈɪntrɪstɪd〕*adj.* 感興趣的 < *in* >

(D) interest〔ˈɪntrɪst〕*n.* 興趣 < *in* >

* **not…at all** 一點也不

fashion〔ˈfæʃən〕*n.* 流行；時尚　　news〔njuz〕*n.* 新聞

15. (**B**) <u>As long as</u> you take enough rest, you will get better.

<u>只要</u>你有足夠的休息，健康情況就會好轉。

as long as 只要 (連接詞片語)

而 (A) although「雖然」，(C) even if「即使」，均不合
句意，(D) that 不能引導副詞子句，故用法不合。

* rest〔rɛst〕*n.* 休息　　**take a rest** 休息
better〔ˈbɛtɚ〕*adj.* (健康情況) 有所好轉的 (well 的比較級)

第二部份：段落填空

Questions 16-20

　　I <u>attend</u> a nice junior high school in Taipei.　My school is
　　　　16
very close to the sea, so in my biology class, we often <u>take</u> trips
　　　　　　　　　　　　　　　　　　　　　　　　　　　17
to the <u>sea</u> to study the fish life.　Students and teachers from other
　　　18
places in Taiwan come to visit my school very often, because it

is a very special school.　We are good in many different <u>subjects</u>,
　　　　　　　　　　　　　　　　　　　　　　　　　　　19
especially math and science.　We have won awards in many

math competitions and science exhibitions.　I'm so proud <u>to be</u>
　　　　　　　　　　　　　　　　　　　　　　　　　　　20
a student at my school.

　　我就讀台北一所很好的國中。我的學校非常靠近海邊，所以上生物
課時，我們常常前往海邊，研究魚類。經常有來自台灣其他地方的學生
跟老師，來參觀我們的學校，因為這是一所非常特別的學校。我們在很
多不同的學科都表現得很好，特別是數理方面。我們在許多數學競賽與
科展都得過獎。我非常以身為這所學校的學生為榮。

close〔klos〕adj. 接近的 < to >
biology〔baɪˋɑlədʒɪ〕n. 生物　　study〔ˋstʌdɪ〕v. 研究
life〔laɪf〕n. 生物　　visit〔ˋvɪzɪt〕v. 參觀
special〔ˋspɛʃəl〕adj. 特別的
different〔ˋdɪfrənt〕adj. 不同的
especially〔əˋspɛʃəlɪ〕adv. 特別是
science〔ˋsaɪəns〕n. 科學　　win〔wɪn〕v. 贏得
award〔əˋwɔrd〕n. 獎　　competition〔͵kɑmpəˋtɪʃən〕n. 比賽
exhibition〔͵ɛksəˋbɪʃən〕n. 展覽

16. (**B**)   (A) arrive〔əˋraɪv〕v. 到達

          (B) ***attend***〔əˋtɛnd〕v. 上（學）

          (C) agree〔əˋgri〕v. 同意

          (D) appear〔əˋpɪr〕v. 出現

17. (**A**)   ***take a trip*** 去旅行（*= make a trip = go on a trip*）

18. (**C**)   依句意，學校靠近海邊，所以生物課到「海」邊研究魚類，

          故選 (C) ***sea***。而 (A) museum〔mjuˋziəm〕n. 博物館，(B)

          mountains〔ˋmauntn̩〕n. 山，(D) sky〔skaɪ〕n. 天空，均

          不合句意。

19. (**D**)   (A) lesson〔ˋlɛsn̩〕n. 課程

          (B) subway〔ˋsʌbˏwe〕n. 地下鐵

          (C) game〔gem〕n. 遊戲；比賽

          (D) ***subject***〔ˋsʌbdʒɪkt〕n. 科目

20. (**A**)   { ***be proud to*** + ***V.*** 以…爲榮；以…爲傲

           be proud of + ***V-ing***

Questions 21-25

No one can learn a language well <u>without</u> a good dictionary.
21
It is an important tool and it will tell you <u>not only</u> what a word
22
means but also how it is used. As a language changes with time,
a good dictionary needs <u>to be changed</u> about every ten years. A
23
good dictionary will tell you many interesting facts, like the
pronunciation and meanings of a word. It will also tell you how a
simple word can be used <u>in</u> different ways. So before you use a
24
dictionary, <u>be</u> sure to read the front part to learn how to use it well.
25

要學好一種語言，沒有一本好的字典是不可能的。它是個重要的工具，它不只會告訴你字的意思，還告訴你字的用法。語言會隨著時間而改變，因此一本好的字典，大概每十年就要改版一次。一本好的字典會告訴你很多有趣的資料，如字的發音跟意思。它也會告訴你一個簡單的字不同的用法。所以當你使用一本字典前，務必先閱讀前言部分，以了解要如何好好的運用。

language〔ˈlæŋgwɪdʒ〕n. 語言
dictionary〔ˈdɪkʃənˌɛrɪ〕n. 字典
important〔ɪmˈpɔrtn̩t〕adj. 重要的　　tool〔tul〕n. 工具
mean〔min〕v. 意思是　　as〔æz〕conj. 因為
change〔tʃendʒ〕v. 改變　　***with time*** 隨著時間
about〔əˈbaut〕prep. 大約　　***every ten years*** 每隔十年
fact〔fækt〕n. 事實　　pronunciation〔prəˌnʌsɪˈeʃən〕n. 發音
meaning〔ˈminɪŋ〕n. 意思　　simple〔ˈsɪmpl̩〕adj. 簡單的
way〔we〕n. 方式　　front〔frʌnt〕adj. 前面的
part〔pɑrt〕n. 部分　　learn〔lɝn〕v. 知道

21. (**D**) 依句意，若是「沒有」好的字典，就無法把語言學好，須用介系詞 *without*，選 (D)。

22. (**A**) *not only…but also~*　不僅…，而且~

23. (**D**) 按照句意，字典需要「被改編」，故用不定詞的被動語態，「to be + p.p.」的形式，選 (D) *to be changed*。

24. (**C**) 「用」~方法，選 (C) *in*。

25. (**C**) 此為祈使句的句型，即以原形動詞開頭，故選 (C) *be sure to + V.*「務必要~」。

第三部份：閱讀理解

Questions 26-27

26. (**A**) 這個告示牌是什麼意思？

  (A) 你必須注意小孩。

  (B) 你必須穿越街道。

  (C) 你可以開快車。

  (D) 你不能單獨行走。

  * sign〔saɪn〕*n.* 告示牌　　watch〔wɑtʃ〕*v.* 注意看＜*for*＞
    cross〔krɔs〕*v.* 穿越　　quickly〔'kwɪklɪ〕*adv.* 快速地
    alone〔ə'lon〕*adv.* 獨自

27. (**B**) 你在哪裡最有可能看到此告示牌？

  (A) 動物園附近。

  (B) 學校附近。

  (C) 機場附近。

  (D) 停車場附近。

  * likely〔'laɪklɪ〕*adv.* 可能
    airport〔'ɛr,port〕*n.* 機場
    parking lot 停車場

Questions 28-30

以下的圖表顯示，不同的年齡層，籃球球迷與羽毛球球迷人數多少的百分比。仔細分析此折線圖，並回答問題。

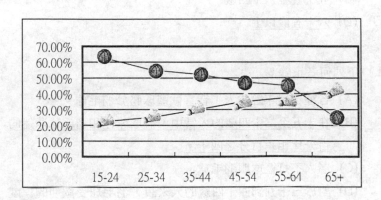

following〔ˋfɑləwɪŋ〕adj. 下列的   chart〔tʃɑrt〕n. 圖表
show〔ʃo〕v 顯示   percentage〔pəˋsɛntɪdʒ〕n. 百分比
fan〔fæn〕n.（電影、運動等的）迷
badminton〔ˋbædmɪntən〕n. 羽毛球   age〔edʒ〕n. 年齡
group〔grup〕n. 群；團體   *age group* 年齡層
graph〔græf〕n. 圖表   *line graph* 折線圖
carefully〔ˋkɛrfəlɪ〕adv. 仔細地

28.（ **A** ）哪個年齡層的籃球迷人數最多？

(A) 十五至二十四歲。　　(B) 三十五至四十四歲。

(C) 五十五至六十四歲。　　(D) 六十五歲以上。

* among〔əˋmʌŋ〕prep. 在…之中
number〔ˋnʌmbɚ〕n. 數量

29. (**D**) 這張圖表顯示，羽毛球在 ＿＿＿＿＿＿ 的年齡層最受
歡迎。

　　(A) 十五至二十四歲

　　(B) 三十五至四十四歲

　　(C) 五十五至六十四歲

　　(D) <u>六十五歲以上</u>

30. (**B**) 下列何者正確？

　　(A) 各種不同年齡的人，皆喜歡籃球勝於羽毛球。

　　(B) <u>在十五至二十四歲的人當中，籃球球迷和羽毛球球迷的
百分比相差百分之四十。</u>

　　(C) 老人不打籃球跟羽毛球。

　　(D) 對於三十五到四十四歲的人來說，羽毛球受歡迎的程度
和籃球相同。

　　* *of all ages* 各種不同年齡的
　　difference〔ˈdɪfərəns〕*n.*（數量）差距
　　point〔pɔɪnt〕*n.* 點數　　*as…as～* 和～一樣…

Questions 31-32

From:	peter7788@hotmail.com
To:	bbecky@aol.com
Subject:	My homepage is coming soon!

Dear Rebecca,

How's everything with you now? Well, I'm now working on my homepage on the Web. I plan to open it on September 1st, and the address of this wonderful site is http://www. gept.idv.tw. You know, a lot of information about music and movies, which are my hobbies, will be available. I also hope to make many links. Why don't you pop in to my page? I can't wait to know your opinions.

Have a nice day!
Peter

寄件者：　peter7788@hotmail.com

收件者：　bbecky@aol.com

主　旨：　My homepage is coming soon!

親愛的蕾貝卡：

妳現在一切還好嗎？嗯，我現在正在架設我的網頁。我預計九月一日上線，這超棒的網站的網址是 http://www.gept.idv.tw。妳知道我的嗜好是音樂與電影，網站上會有很多這方面的資訊。我希望會有很多的友站連結。妳何不瀏覽一下我的網站？我迫不及待想知道妳的意見。

祝妳有美好的一天！

彼得

---

subject〔'sʌbdʒɪkt〕*n.* 主題

homepage〔'hom'pedʒ〕*n.* 網站首頁　　***work on*** 致力於

Web〔wɛb〕*n.* 網路（= *Internet* = *Net*）

plan〔plæn〕*v.* 計畫　　　open〔'opən〕*v.* 開放

address〔ə'drɛs〕*n.* 地址（這裡指「網址」）

wonderful〔'wʌndəfəl〕*adj.* 很棒的

site〔saɪt〕*n.* 網站（= *website*）

information〔,ɪnfə'meʃən〕*n.* 資訊　　hobby〔'hɑbɪ〕*n.* 嗜好

available〔ə'veləbḷ〕*adj.* 可獲得的　　link〔lɪŋk〕*n.* 連結

pop in 順道拜訪　　page〔pedʒ〕*n.* 網站首頁（指 homepage）

can't wait to + *V.* 等不及要~　　opinion〔ə'pɪnjən〕*n.* 意見

31. (**C**) 關於彼得的網頁，何者正確？

  (A) 網頁是關於他的學校生活。

  (B) 網頁已經開放了四個月。

  (C) 網頁預定在九月開放。

  (D) 網頁有關於學英文的資訊。

  * schedule〔ˈskɛdʒul〕v. 預定

32. (**A**) 電子郵件裡的片語 "pop in" 意思是 _____。

  (A) 拜訪　　　　　　　(B) 發出聲音

  (C) 跳躍　　　　　　　(D) 預看

  * phrase〔frez〕n. 片語　　e-mail〔ˈiˌmel〕n. 電子郵件
    sound〔saund〕n. 聲音　　jump〔dʒʌmp〕v. 跳
    preview〔ˈpriˌvju〕v. 預看

Questions 33-35

Do you know the story about where the word "hamburger" came from? Almost a hundred years ago, some Germans came to the United States. One day when they were cooking some round pieces of beef, some Americans saw them and asked them what they were making. Because those Germans did not understand the question, they thought the Americans were asking them where they came from. They answered, "Hamburg."

你知道「漢堡」這個字的由來嗎？大約在一百年前，有些德國人來到了美國。有一天，當他們在煮一些圓形牛肉片的時候，有些美國人看到，就問他們在煮什麼。因爲那些德國人聽不懂問題，以爲美國人在問他們是哪裡來的，於是他們就回答：「漢堡。」

hamburger〔'hæmbɝgɚ〕n. 漢堡
almost〔'ɔl,most〕adv. 幾乎　　German〔'dʒɝmən〕n. 德國人
one day 有一天　　　round〔raʊnd〕adj. 圓形的
piece〔pis〕n. 片　　beef〔bif〕n. 牛肉
understand〔,ʌndɚ'stænd〕v. 了解
Hamburg〔'hæmbɝg〕n. 漢堡（德國的城市）

One of the Americans was a restaurant owner. He knew that many Americans loved to eat sandwiches, so he put the round pieces of cooked beef in buns. He called his sandwiches hamburgers. Today, hamburgers are still very popular in fast-food restaurants and people around the world know what hamburgers are.

這些美國人當中，有一個是餐廳老闆。他知道很多美國人愛吃三明治，他就把煎好的圓形牛肉片夾在小圓麵包裡。他稱這種三明治爲漢堡。現在，漢堡在速食店仍然很受歡迎，而且全世界的人都知道漢堡是什麼。

restaurant〔ˋrɛstərənt〕*n.* 餐廳　　owner〔ˋonə〕*n.* 老闆

sandwich〔ˋsændwɪtʃ〕*n.* 三明治

cooked〔kʊkt〕*adj.* 煮好的

bun〔bʌn〕*n.* 小圓麵包（這裡是指漢堡包）

call〔kɔl〕*v.* 稱　　popular〔ˋpɑpjələ〕*adj.* 受歡迎的

fast-food restaurant 速食店　　***around the world*** 在全世界

33. (**D**) 誰先製造漢堡的？

　　(A) 漢堡先生。　　　　　(B) 一位在漢堡的美國人。

　　(C) 德國先生。　　　　　(D) <u>開餐廳的一位美國人。</u>

　　* own〔on〕*v.* 擁有

34. (**C**) 從本文，我們可以知道早期的漢堡沒有 ＿＿＿＿＿＿＿＿。

　　(A) 麵包　　　　　　　　(B) 牛肉

　　(C) <u>火腿</u>　　　　　　　　(D) 小圓麵包

　　* passage〔ˋpæsɪdʒ〕*n.*（文章等的）一節；一段

　　　times〔taɪmz〕*n. pl.*（特定的）時期

　　　ham〔hæm〕*n.* 火腿

35. (**D**) 下列敘述何者正確？

　　(A) 漢堡是美國一個城市的名字。

　　(B) 德國人知道美國人喜歡牛肉。

　　(C) 並沒有很多人喜歡在速食店點漢堡。

　　(D) <u>這些德國人並不清楚了解美國人所問的問題的意思。</u>

　　* clearly〔ˋklɪrlɪ〕*adv.* 清楚地

三、寫作能力測驗

第一部份：單句寫作

第1~5題：句子改寫

1. Paula asked me, "Could you lend me your umbrella?"
   Paula asked me if ＿＿＿＿＿＿ lend her my umbrella.

　　重點結構：直接問句改為間接問句的用法

　　　解　答：<u>Paula asked me if I could lend her my umbrella.</u>

　　句型分析：Paula asked me + if + 主詞 + 動詞

　　　說　明：Could you lend me your umbrella? 是直接問句，
　　　　　　　現在要放在 if「是否」後面，做為 Paula asked me
　　　　　　　的受詞，即名詞子句（間接問句）「連接詞 + 主詞
　　　　　　　+ 動詞」的形式，在 Paula asked me 後面接 if I
　　　　　　　could lend her my umbrella，並把問號改成句點。

　　* lend〔lɛnd〕v. 借（出）　　umbrella〔ʌmˈbrɛlə〕n. 雨傘

2. Frank is taller than all the other students in his class.
   Frank ＿＿＿＿＿＿ tallest ＿＿＿＿＿＿ in his class.

　　重點結構：比較級表達最高級的用法

　　　解　答：<u>Frank is the tallest student in his class.</u>

　　句型分析：主詞 + be 動詞 + the + 形容詞最高級 + 名詞

　　　說　明：題目的意思是「法蘭克比他班上的其他學生高」，
　　　　　　　換句話說，「法蘭克是他班上最高的學生」，可以
　　　　　　　用最高級表達，在 tallest 之前須加定冠詞 the，並
　　　　　　　把 students 改為單數名詞 student。

3. Andy overslept, so he was late for school.

   Andy ＿＿＿＿＿＿＿＿ because ＿＿＿＿＿＿＿＿＿＿.

   重點結構：because 的用法

   解　答：Andy was late for school because he overslept.

   句型分析：主詞｜動詞 + because + 主詞 + 動詞

   說　明：連接詞 so（所以）和 because（因為）的比較：

   $\begin{cases} \text{原因 + so + 結果} \\ \text{結果 + because + 原因} \end{cases}$

   * oversleep〔'ovə'slip〕v. 睡過頭　　late〔let〕adj. 遲到的

4. Matt will go to junior high school.

   When ＿＿＿＿＿＿＿＿＿＿＿＿＿＿＿＿＿＿＿＿＿?

   重點結構：未來式的 wh-問句

   解　答：When will Matt go to junior high school?

   句型分析：When + will + 主詞 + 原形動詞？

   說　明：這一題應將未來式直述句改為 wh-問句，疑問詞後面
   要加表未來的助動詞 will。

5. Nancy watches cartoons every night.

   Nancy ＿＿＿＿＿＿＿＿＿＿＿＿＿＿＿ last night.

   重點結構：過去式動詞

   解　答：Nancy watched cartoons last night.

   句型分析：主詞 + 動詞 + 時間副詞

   說　明：時間副詞 every night 改為 last night，動詞要改為
   過去式，watches 改成 watched。

   * cartoon〔kar'tun〕n. 卡通

第6～10題：句子合併

6. May likes to listen to music.
   May also likes to go climbing.
   May likes to _____.

   重點結構：and 的用法
   　解　答：May likes to listen to music and (to) go climbing.
   　　　　　或 May likes to go climbing and (to) listen to music.
   句型分析：主詞 + 動詞 + 不定詞 + and + 不定詞或原形動詞
   　説　明：and 是對等連接詞，連接兩個不定詞，做動詞 likes
   　　　　　的受詞，而第二個不定詞的 to 可省略。

   　*** go climbing*** 去爬山

7. How much does it cost?
   I don't know.
   I don't know how _____.

   重點結構：間接問句做名詞子句
   　解　答：I don't know how much it costs.
   句型分析：I don't know + how + 主詞 + 動詞
   　説　明：在 wh-問句前加 I don't know，形成間接問句，即
   　　　　　「疑問詞 + 主詞 + 動詞」的形式，必須把動詞 cost
   　　　　　放在最後面，因為 it 是第三人稱單數，故 cost 須加
   　　　　　s，並把問號改成句點。

8. Tim has cats.

Eva is Tim's cat.

Eva _____ one of _____.

重點結構：「one of ＋所有格＋複數名詞」的用法

解　答：<u>Eva is one of Tim's cats.</u>

句型分析：主詞＋be 動詞＋one of ＋所有格＋複數名詞

說　明：題目的意思是「伊娃是提姆的貓當中的一隻」，「～當中的一個」用「one of ＋複數名詞」來表示，cat 須用複數形。

9. Fred is 155cm tall.

Robert is 155cm tall, too.

Fred _____ as Robert.

重點結構：「as…as～」的用法

解　答：<u>Fred is as tall as Robert.</u>

句型分析：主詞＋be 動詞＋as ＋形容詞＋as ＋受詞

說　明：這題是說佛瑞德身高一百五十五公分，羅伯特身高也是一百五十五公分，所以兩個人長得一樣高，用「as…as～」來連接兩句話，表「和～一樣…」。

* cm 公分（*centimeter* 的略稱）

10. Judy goes jogging.

Then, she has breakfast.

Judy _____ before _____.

重點結構：before 的用法

解　答：Judy goes jogging before she has breakfast.

或 Judy goes jogging before (having) breakfast.

句型分析：主詞＋動詞＋before＋主詞＋動詞

或 主詞＋動詞＋before＋（動）名詞

說　明：then「然後」表示茱蒂先慢跑，再吃早餐，現在用
before「在～之前」來表示事情的先後順序。而
before 有兩種詞性，若作為連接詞，引導副詞子句
時，須接完整的主詞與動詞，即 before she has
breakfast；若作為介系詞，後面須接名詞或動名
詞，即 before breakfast 或 before having
breakfast。

＊ *go jogging* 去慢跑

第 11～15 題：重組

11. Kelly _____.

been learning / has / for / karate / seven years

重點結構：現在完成進行式字序

解　答：Kelly has been learning karate for seven years.

句型分析：主詞＋have/has been＋現在分詞＋for＋一段時間

說　明：現在完成進行式的結構是「主詞＋have/has been
＋現在分詞」，而「for＋一段時間」，表「持續
（多久）」，此時間片語置於句尾。

＊ karate〔kəˋrɑtɪ〕*n.* 空手道

12. He _____.
   to make / with / my brother / wants / friends

   重點結構：「make friends with *sb.*」的用法

   解　答：He wants to make friends with my brother.

   句型分析：主詞十動詞＋不定詞片語

   說　明：make friends with *sb.* 表「與某人交朋友」。

13. Iris bought _____.
   at the bookstore / this pencil box / the park / next to

   重點結構：表地點的介系詞的用法

   解　答：Iris bought this pencil box at the bookstore
   next to the park.

   句型分析：主詞＋動詞＋受詞十地方副詞

   說　明：next to the park 修飾 bookstore。

   * *pencil box* 鉛筆盒　　bookstore〔'buk͵stor〕*n.* 書店
   next to 在…旁邊

14. How many _____?
   in the basket / are / eggs / there

   重點結構：「How many + 複數名詞 + are there?」的用法

   解　答：How many eggs are there in the basket?

   句型分析：How many + 複數名詞 + are there + 地方副詞

   說　明：「How many + 複數名詞？」表「～有多少？」，而
   「there + be 動詞」表「有」，在問句中要倒裝，
   故形成 are there，地方副詞 in the basket 則置於
   句尾。

   * egg〔ɛg〕*n.* 蛋　　basket〔'bæskɪt〕*n.* 籃子

15. The _____.
    and / sweet / tastes / sour / soup

> 重點結構：「taste + 形容詞」的用法
>
> 解　答：<u>The soup tastes sour and sweet.</u>
>
> 　　　或 <u>The soup tastes sweet and sour.</u>
>
> 句型分析：主詞 + 動詞 + 形容詞
>
> 說　明：動詞 taste「嚐起來」後面須接形容詞做補語，用對
> 　　　　等連接詞 and 連接兩個形容詞。
>
> * soup〔sup〕n. 湯　　taste〔test〕v. 嚐起來
>
>   sweet〔swit〕adj. 甜的　　sour〔saur〕adj. 酸的

第二部份：段落寫作

題目：爸爸買了一輛新腳踏車給我，並且教我如何騎腳踏車。經過
　　　不斷的嚐試，我終於學會了。請根據圖片內容寫一篇約 50 字
　　　的簡短描述。

My father gave me a new bike. I was very happy. ***But*** I didn't know how to ride it. My father tried very hard to teach me. I tried again and again, ***but*** I could not do it. I even fell and hurt my knee. I hated the new bike.

My father asked me to try one more time. ***To my surprise***, I could ride the bike. I was very happy, and my father was happy, too.

bike〔baɪk〕*n.* 腳踏車　　hard〔hɑrd〕*adv.* 努力地
ride〔raɪd〕*v.* 騎　　***again and again*** 一再地
fall〔fɔl〕*v.* 跌落（三態變化爲：fall-fell-fallen）
hurt〔hɝt〕*v.* 使受傷（三態同形）　　knee〔ni〕*n.* 膝蓋
hate〔het〕*v.* 討厭　　***ask sb. + to V.*** 要求某人做～
to one's surprise 令某人驚訝的是

心得筆記欄................

全民英語能力分級檢定測驗
初級測驗③

一、聽力測驗

本測驗分三部份，全爲三選一之選擇題，每部份各 10 題，共 30 題，作答時間約 20 分鐘。

第一部份：看圖辨義

本部份共 10 題，試題冊上每題有一個圖片，請聽錄音機播出一個相關的問題，與 A、B、C 三個英語敘述後，選一個與所看到圖片最相符的答案，並在答案紙上相對的圓圈內塗黑作答。每題播出一遍，問題及選項均不印在試題冊上。

例：（看）

（聽）

Look at the picture.　How much is the hamburger?

A.　It's eighty dollars.

B.　It's fifty-five dollars.

C.　It's eighteen dollars.

正確答案爲 A

Question 1

Question 2

Question 3

Question 4

Question 5

Question 6

請 翻 頁 ⟹

Question 7

Question 8

Question 9

Question 10

請 翻 頁

第二部份：問答

　　　　本部份共 10 題，每題錄音機會播出一個問句或直述句，
　　　　每題播出一次，聽後請從試題冊上 A、B、C 三個選項中，
　　　　選出一個最適合的回答或回應，並在答案紙上塗黑作答。

　　　例：

　　（聽）Good morning, Kevin. How are you?

　　（看）A.　I'm fine, thank you.
　　　　　B.　I'm in the living room.
　　　　　C.　My name is Kevin.

　　　　正確答案為 A

11. A. You're welcome.
　　 B. I'd love to come.
　　 C. Here you are.

12. A. Sure. That'll be
　　　　50 dollars.
　　 B. Of course. Here it is.
　　 C. No thanks, I don't
　　　　need one.

13. A. A small town near
　　　　Taipei.
　　 B. The supermarket.
　　 C. To the park.

14. A. I like apples.
　　 B. Fruit is good for you.
　　 C. Yes, I would.

15. A. No. You should take
       number 57.
    B. Yes, the museum is
       open today.
    C. No, I don't like
       going to the museum.

16. A. I will. Thanks for
       warning me.
    B. I'm sorry. It was an
       accident.
    C. I can't catch it.

17. A. Very well, thank
       you.
    B. On Fourth Avenue.
    C. I was born in Tainan.

18. A. Yes, it's a beautiful
       day.
    B. I hope it clears up
       soon.
    C. You're right. There's
       not a could in the sky.

19. A. On the fifteenth of
       the month.
    B. It's in the sky.
    C. The full moon is
       round.

20. A. I see them on the
       table.
    B. I can't see without
       them.
    C. The glass is too dirty
       to see through.

請 翻 頁 ▌⟹

第三部份： 簡短對話

本部份共 10 題，每題錄音機會播出一段對話及一個相關的問題，每題播出兩次，聽後請從試題冊上 A、B、C 三個選項中，選出一個最適合的回答，並在答案紙上塗黑作答。

例：

（聽） (Woman) Good afternoon, ...Mr. Davis?

(Man) Yes.　I have an appointment with Dr. Sanders at two o'clock.　My son Tommy has a fever.

(Woman) Oh, that's too bad.　Well, please have a seat, Mr. Davis.　Dr. Sanders will be right with you.

Question: Where did this conversation take place?

（看） A. In a post office.

B. In a restaurant.

C. In a doctor's office.

正確答案為 C

21. A. In junior high school.
   B. In elementary school.
   C. He doesn't meet Steve anymore.

22. A. Fourteen.
   B. Twelve.
   C. Sixteen.

23. A. He is admiring a garden.
    B. He is taking a picture.
    C. He is exercising.

24. A. She will pay fifty dollars.
    B. She will pay one hundred dollars.
    C. She will buy twelve apples.

25. A. Fifty dollars.
    B. His pen.
    C. The girl's wallet.

26. A. He will tell the girl the time.
    B. He will not go to his class.
    C. He will give the girl a hand.

27. A. She is going to eat at her grandparents' house.
    B. She doesn't want to see her grandparents.
    C. Her grandparents will visit her.

28. A. He has also been interested in the stars for a long time.
    B. He will look for a club that he has always been interested in.
    C. He will join the Astronomy Club, too.

29. A. In the train station.
    B. It departs at 3:20.
    C. At a quarter after three.

30. A. It got lost.
    B. It was run over.
    C. It lives in the elementary school.

請 翻 頁

二、閱讀能力測驗

本測驗分三部份，全為四選一之選擇題，共 35 題，作答時間 35 分鐘。

第一部份：詞彙和結構

本部份共 15 題，每題含一個空格。請就試題冊上 A、B、C、D 四個選項中選出最適合題意的字或詞，標示在答案紙上。

1. The drunk driver is _____ for the serious accident.
   A. fluent
   B. jealous
   C. responsible
   D. greedy

2. The weather was so hot that the paper fan was not very _____.
   A. changeable
   B. effective
   C. formal
   D. funny

3. Nancy hates all _____, especially roaches.
   A. bugs
   B. bags
   C. belts
   D. burgers

4. Cathy hid the candy in her right hand. Then she held out both hands and asked her brother to _____ where the candy was.
   A. raise
   B. clap
   C. shake
   D. guess

5. Today is my birthday, so my good friend will _____ me to a movie.
   A. treat
   B. examine
   C. reply
   D. collect

6. Little Wendy cried loudly after bumping _____ the table.
   A. in
   B. into
   C. to
   D. on

7. Carl worked at the bookstore last month, but he doesn't work there _____.
   A. again
   B. anymore
   C. anyway
   D. anywhere

請 翻 頁 ⟹

8. _____ you go to the baseball game next Friday evening?

   A. Have

   B. Are

   C. Can

   D. Did

9. My parents do the housework during the week, but I help
   _____ on the weekend.

   A. it

   B. her

   C. him

   D. them

10. We hurried into the building because it _____ raining
    harder and harder.

    A. was

    B. were

    C. has been

    D. will be

11. I'm sorry. I _____ go to your birthday party next
    Wednesday.

    A. can

    B. can't

    C. should

    D. shouldn't

12. Most of the young girls _____ live in Taipei like to go
shopping at the big department stores on holidays.
A. which
B. when
C. who
D. where

13. Andy : Wow! There are so many dolls in this shop!
Patty : Yes, I like those red _____. How about you?
A. them
B. one
C. ones
D. some

14. Our team lost the game. We played _____ this time.
A. bad
B. badly
C. poor
D. worst

15. The first question is _____ than the second question.
A. easy
B. more easier
C. easier
D. more easy

請 翻 頁 ◖⟹

第二部份：段落填空

　　本部份共 10 題，包括二個段落，每個段落各含 5 個空格。
　　請就試題冊上 A、B、C、D 四個選項中選出最適合題意
　　的字或詞，標示在答案紙上。

Questions 16-20

　　A doctor and an art teacher loved the same pretty woman
___(16)___ in their apartment building. One spring vacation, the
teacher ___(17)___ to take his students to the country. The night
before he left, he gave the girl a(n) ___(18)___ and told her, "I'll
be away for a week. I have a present for you. Open it after I
___(19)___." When the girl opened it, she found seven apples
and this ___(20)___ : "An apple a day keeps the doctor away."

16. A. that living
　　B. who lived
　　C. to live
　　D. live

17. A. asked
　　B. was asking
　　C. be asked
　　D. was asked

18. A. toy
　　B. apple
　　C. envelope
　　D. box

19. A. leave
　　B. left
　　C. will leave
　　D. leaving

20. A. fruit
　　B. answer
　　C. example
　　D. note

Questions 21-25

I bought my son a dog called Lassie last year. Dogs are children's friends. Mike had had no friends at ___(21)___ before Lassie ___(22)___. Now, he enjoys ___(23)___ with her every day. "Lassie is cute and she is my best friend!" Mike is a happy boy now.

Mike can learn how to be kind to others. We ___(24)___ him how to get along with Lassie. He is now more polite to animals, and to other people!

Children love dogs and dogs love children. So why not put them together and let them ___(25)___ a good time?

21. A. once
    B. all
    C. night
    D. last

22. A. comes
    B. came
    C. come
    D. were coming

23. A. playing
    B. to play
    C. to playing
    D. play

24. A. taught
    B. made
    C. answered
    D. asked

25. A. having
    B. has
    C. to have
    D. have

請 翻 頁 ◖◗⟹

第三部份： 閱讀理解

本部份共 10 題，包括數段短文，每段短文後有 1～3 個相關問題，請就試題冊上 A、B、C、D 四個選項中選出最適合者，標示在答案紙上。

Questions 26-28

Answer the questions according to the train schedule.

TRAIN SCHEDULE

Train Number Station　Departure	1001	1003	1009	1015
Taipei	06:06	07:00	08:40	13:05
Taichung	09:08	09:16	10:40	15:05
Changhua	09:36	09:43	—	—
Chiayi	10:46	10:27	11:43	—
Tainan	11:50	11:08	12:22	16:43
Kaohsiung	12:45	11:39	12:52	17:14

26. Which is the fastest train from Taipei to Kaohsiung?

    A. 1001.

    B. 1003.

    C. 1009.

    D. 1015.

27. Karen lives in Taipei. She wants to go to Changhua to visit her grandparents. Which trains should she **NOT** take?

    A. 1001 and 1003.

    B. 1003 and 1009.

    C. 1009 and 1015.

    D. 1003 and 1015.

28. Which trains make the most stops?

    A. 1001 and 1003.

    B. 1003 and 1009.

    C. 1009 and 1015.

    D. 1003 and 1015.

請 翻 頁 ⬛⇨

Questions 29-30

ANDY LEE
LIVE CONCERT

Date : December 20, 2002
Time : 8:00 pm — 9:30 pm
Location : NTU Sports Center, Taipei
Ticket Prices : NT$500, NT$900, NT$1200
Hotline : 0800-088-812

29. What can we do if we have any questions about the concert?

A. Send a letter.

B. Send an e-mail.

C. Send a fax.

D. Make a phone call.

30. Which of the following is true?

A. Andy Lee will give two concerts in Taipei.

B. There are four different kinds of tickets.

C. The concert will last two hours.

D. The concert will be held in December.

<u>Questions 31-33</u>

Mr. Lee is a farmer. He works on his farm every day. It is very hot on the farm. So when he takes a rest, he usually sits under a tree because it is cooler there.

A few days ago, Mr. Lee saw a rabbit. The rabbit was running very fast. Then it hit a tree and died. Mr. Lee was very happy because he had a rabbit. He thought, "Soon I'll have a lot more rabbits. I'll sell them in the market. Soon I'll have a lot of money. I'll never have to work hard in the field anymore." He decided to sit under the tree to wait for more rabbits.

He has sat under the tree for more than one week, but no rabbits have hit the tree. He doesn't know that the same thing will not happen if he just sits and waits.

31. How did the rabbit die?
    A. It was killed by the farmer.
    B. It was killed by a hunter.
    C. It was running so fast that it hit a tree and died.
    D. The weather was so hot that it died.

請 翻 頁 ◖⇒

32. What does the farmer want the rabbits for?

   A. He wants to eat them all by himself.

   B. He wants to eat them with his family.

   C. He wants to sell them for money.

   D. He wants to give them to his friends.

33. What is the lesson of this story?

   A. Rabbits are stupid.

   B. People don't need to work hard if they are lucky.

   C. Rabbits are not lucky.

   D. Lazy people are stupid.

Questions 34-35

August 16, 2002

Dear Ms. Huang,

I'm writing this letter to you because my son, Frank Wu, who is in your class, cannot go to school today.

This morning, when he woke up, he did not feel very well. We went to see a doctor and he was given some medicine. The doctor said that he had to stay at home for one or two days. My wife and I will let him go back to school when he feels better.

Thank you very much.

Yours truly,
Tony Wu

34. Why **CAN'T** Frank go to school?
    A. His mother is sick.
    B. He is sick.
    C. He woke up late.
    D. He is lazy.

35. Who is Ms. Huang?
    A. Frank's doctor.
    B. Frank's teacher.
    C. Frank's mother.
    D. Tony Wu's teacher.

請 翻 頁 ◀▯▭▷

三、寫作能力測驗

　　本測驗共有兩部份,第一部份為單句寫作,第二部份為段落寫作。測驗時間為 40 分鐘。

第一部份： 單句寫作

　　　　　　請將答案寫在寫作能力測驗答案紙對應的題號旁,如有拼字、標點、大小寫之錯誤,將予扣分。

第 1~5 題： 句子改寫

　　　　　　請依題目之提示,將原句改寫成指定型式,並將改寫的句子完整地寫在答案紙上(包括提示之文字及標點符號)。

1. Two boys are playing badminton at the playground.

　　Who _____?

2. Eating too much is bad for your health.

　　It is _____.

3. I eat and sleep a lot.

　　_____ last weekend.

4. My parents bought some comic books for me.

　　My parents _____ comic books.

5. "I like your new shoes," I said to Mary.

　　I said to Mary that _____.

第6～10題：句子合併

　　　　請依照題目指示，將兩句合併成一句，並將合併的句子
　　　　完整地寫在答案紙上（包括提示之文字及標點符號）。

6. Polly can't speak Japanese.

   Rita can't speak Japanese.

   Neither _____.

7. Kevin is very young.

   Kevin cannot go to school.

   Kevin is too _____.

8. I have a sister.

   My sister's name is Jennifer.

   I have _____ Jennifer.

9. I like to eat peanut butter very much.

   My brother doesn't like to eat peanut butter.

   I like _____ peanut butter very much, _____ it.

10. Bob is fixing his computer.

    Nancy helps him.

    Nancy helps _____.

請 翻 頁 ⟹

第 11～15 題：重組

　　　　請將題目中所有提示字詞整合成一有意義的句子，並
　　　　將重組的句子完整地寫在答案紙上（包括提示之文字
　　　　及標點符號）。答案中必須使用所有提示字詞，且不
　　　　能隨意增加字詞，否則不予計分。

11. What _____?
   Kelly / her / do / like / animals / and / mother

12. I _____.
   at all / orange / don't / juice / like

13. David _____.
   best / is / one / friends / my / of

14. Sandra _____.
   earthquake / when / watching / the / happened / was / TV

15. Please _____.
   page / turn to / seven / number

第二部份：段落寫作

題目： 上星期天，我們全家出遊到山上野餐（have a picnic），請根據
　　　圖片內容寫一篇約 50 字的簡短描述。

初級英檢模擬試題③詳解

一、聽力測驗

Look at the picture for question 1.

1. (**A**) What game do they like to play?
　　　A. They like badminton.
　　　B. They want to play tennis.
　　　C. They are winning.

　　　* badminton (ˈbædmɪntən) *n.* 羽毛球
　　　　tennis (ˈtɛnɪs) *n.* 網球　　win (wɪn) *v.* 獲勝

Look at the picture for question 2.

2. (**B**) What is it?
　　　A. It is a tricycle.　　　B. It is a scooter.
　　　C. It is parked.

　　　* tricycle (ˈtraɪsɪkḷ) *n.* 三輪車
　　　　scooter (ˈskutɚ) *n.* 速克達機車　　park (pɑrk) *v.* 停放

Look at the picture for question 3.

3. (**C**) Where are they?
　　　A. They are in a flower shop.
　　　B. They are celebrating.
　　　C. They are on a stage.

　　　* *flower shop* 花店　　celebrate (ˈsɛləˌbret) *v.* 慶祝
　　　　stage (stedʒ) *n.* 舞台

Look at the picture for question 4.

4. (**C**) How many people are on the roof?
   A. There is one firefighter.
   B. There are seven.
   C. There are four.

   * roof〔ruf〕*n.* 屋頂
   firefighter〔'faɪr͵faɪtɚ〕*n.* 消防隊員（= *fireman*）

Look at the picture for question 5.

5. (**B**) What is the boy doing?
   A. He is putting his shoes away.
   B. He is buying new shoes.
   C. He is making shoes.

   * *put away* 收拾　make〔mek〕*v.* 製作

Look at the picture for question 6.

6. (**A**) Why is she crying?
   A. She slipped on a banana peel.
   B. She cannot peel her banana.
   C. She lost her banana.

   * slip〔slɪp〕*v.* 滑一跤
   banana〔bə'nænə〕*n.* 香蕉
   peel〔pil〕*n.* 皮　*v.* 剝皮　lose〔luz〕*v.* 遺失

Look at the picture for question 7.

7. (**B**) Where is the woman going?

　　　　A. She is going to make a wish.

　　　　B. She is going to the temple.

　　　　C. She has four.

　　　　* wish〔wɪʃ〕*n.* 願望　***make a wish*** 許願
　　　　　temple〔'tɛmpl̩〕*n.* 寺廟

Look at the picture for question 8.

8. (**B**) What kind of race is it?

　　　　A. It is a music contest.

　　　　B. It is a dragon boat race.

　　　　C. It is a snake race.

　　　　* race〔res〕*n.* 比賽　contest〔'kɑntɛst〕*n.* 比賽
　　　　　dragon〔'drægən〕*n.* 龍　boat〔bot〕*n.* 船
　　　　　dragon boat 龍舟　snake〔snek〕*n.* 蛇

Look at the picture for question 9.

9. (**C**) How does the boy feel?

　　　　A. He is getting a shot.

　　　　B. He is very happy to get well.

　　　　C. He is afraid.

　　　　* shot〔ʃɑt〕*n.* 注射；打針
　　　　　get well 康復　afraid〔ə'fred〕*adj.* 害怕的

Look at the picture for question 10.

10. (**C**) How many children are playing in the sand?

    A. The girls are.

    B. It is too hot.

    C. There are four.

    * sand〔sænd〕*n.* 沙子　　***play in the sand*** 玩沙

第二部份

11. (**B**) I'd like to invite you to dinner tomorrow.

    A. You're welcome.

    B. I'd love to come.

    C. Here you are.

    * ***would like to*** + *V.* 想要

      (= *would love to* + *V.* = *want to* + *V.*)

    invite〔ɪn'vaɪt〕*v.* 邀請　　***You're welcome.*** 不客氣。

    Here you are. 你要的東西在這裡；拿去吧。

    (= *Here you go.* = *Here it is.*)

12. (**B**) Could you lend me your eraser?

    A. Sure. That'll be 50 dollars.

    B. Of course. Here it is.

    C. No thanks, I don't need one.

    * lend〔lɛnd〕*v.* 借（出）　　eraser〔ɪ'resɚ〕*n.* 橡皮擦

    Sure. 當然。(= *Of course.*)

    Here it is. 拿去吧。　　need〔nid〕*v.* 需要

13. (**A**) Where are you from?

    A. A small town near Taipei.

    B. The supermarket.

    C. To the park.

    * **be from** 在…長大 (= *grow up in*)
    supermarket ('supɚˌmarkɪt) *n.* 超級市場

14. (**C**) Would you like some fruit?

    A. I like apples.

    B. Fruit is good for you.

    C. Yes, I would.

    * fruit (frut) *n.* 水果   **be good for** 對~有益

15. (**A**) Does this bus go to the museum?

    A. No. You should take number 57.

    B. Yes, the museum is open today.

    C. No, I don't like going to the museum.

    * museum (mju'ziəm) *n.* 博物館
    open ('opən) *adj.* 開放的

16. (**A**) Be careful. The floor is slippery.

    A. I will. Thanks for warning me.

    B. I'm sorry. It was an accident.

    C. I can't catch it.

    * careful ('kɛrfəl) *adj.* 小心的   floor (flor) *n.* 地板
    slippery ('slɪpərɪ) *adj.* 滑的   warn (wɔrn) *v.* 警告
    accident ('æksədənt) *n.* 意外
    catch (kætʃ) *v.* 理解；聽清楚

17. (**B**) Where do you live?

  A. Very well, thank you.

  B. On Fourth Avenue.

  C. I was born in Tainan.

  * avenue〔'ævə,nju〕*n.* 大街；大道
  be born 出生 ***Tainan*** 台南

18. (**C**) There are a lot of stars in the sky tonight.

  A. Yes, it's a beautiful day.

  B. I hope it clears up soon.

  C. You're right. There's not a cloud in the sky.

  * star〔stɑr〕*n.* 星星 sky〔skaɪ〕*n.* 天空
  clear up 放晴 cloud〔klaʊd〕*n.* 雲

19. (**A**) When is the full moon?

  A. On the fifteenth of the month.

  B. It's in the sky.

  C. The full moon is round.

  * ***full moon*** 滿月 month〔mʌnθ〕*n.* 月
  round〔raʊnd〕*adj.* 圓的

20. (**A**) Have you seen my glasses?

  A. I see them on the table.

  B. I can't see without them.

  C. The glass is too dirty to see through.

  * glasses〔'glæsɪz〕*n. pl.* 眼鏡
  without〔wɪð'aʊt〕*prep.* 沒有 glass〔glæs〕*n.* 玻璃
  too…to ~ 太…以致於不~ dirty〔'dɝtɪ〕*adj.* 髒的
  through〔θru〕*prep.* 穿過；透過

第三部份

21. (**B**) W : Do you know Steve?

M : Sure. We've been friends since elementary school.

W : Do you talk to him often?

M : No. Not since we entered different junior high schools.

Question : Where did the man first meet Steve?

 A. In junior high school.

 B. In elementary school.

 C. He doesn't meet Steve anymore.

 * since〔sɪns〕*prep. conj.* 自從

   elementary school 小學　　enter〔ˈɛntɚ〕*v.* 進入

   junior high school 國中　　meet〔mit〕*v.* 認識；遇見

   not…anymore 不再

22. (**C**) M : Do you have any brothers or sisters?

W : Yes. I have a younger brother.

M : How old is he?

W : He's fourteen.

Question : How old might the girl be?

 A. Fourteen.

 B. Twelve.

 C. Sixteen.

 * ***younger brother*** 弟弟

23. (**B**) W : Where should I stand? Here?

M : Move a little to your right so that I can see the garden, too.

W : Like this?

M : Perfect. It's a great shot. Now smile.

Question : What is the man doing?

A. He is admiring a garden.

B. He is taking a picture.

C. He is exercising.

* move〔muv〕v. 移動   *a little* 一點
right〔raɪt〕n. 右邊   *so that* 以便於 (表目的)
garden〔'gɑrdn̩〕n. 花園   perfect〔'pɜfɪkt〕adj. 完美的
shot〔ʃɑt〕n. 鏡頭   smile〔smaɪl〕v. 微笑
admire〔əd'maɪr〕v. 欣賞   *take a picture* 拍照
exercise〔'ɛksə‚saɪz〕v. 運動

24. (**B**) W : Excuse me, how much are the apples?

M : Six for fifty dollars.

W : I'll take twelve.

Question : How much will the woman pay for the apples?

A. She will pay fifty dollars.

B. She will pay one hundred dollars.

C. She will buy twelve apples.

* take〔tek〕v. 買   *pay for* 付錢買

25. (**A**) W：Can you lend me 50 dollars?

　　　　　M：I guess so. What's it for?

　　　　　W：I need a new pen and I left my wallet at home.

　　　　　M：No problem. Here you are.

　　　Question：What did the boy give the girl?

　　　A. Fifty dollars.

　　　B. His pen.

　　　C. The girl's wallet.

　　　* guess〔gɛs〕v. 猜想　　for 表「用途」。
　　　leave〔liv〕v. 遺留　　wallet〔'wɑlɪt〕n. 皮夾
　　　No problem. 沒問題。　　***Here you are.*** 拿去吧。

26. (**C**) W：Do you have time to help me with this?

　　　　　M：Sure. I don't have to go to class for another hour.

　　　　　W：Thanks. I really appreciate it.

　　　Question：What will the boy do?

　　　A. He will tell the girl the time.

　　　B. He will not go to his class.

　　　C. He will give the girl a hand.

　　　* ***help*** *sb.* ***with*** *+ N.* 幫某人做~
　　　appreciate〔ə'priʃɪ,et〕v. 感謝
　　　give *sb.* ***a hand*** 幫助某人 (*= do sb. a favor = help sb.*)

27. (**C**) M : Why don't we go to McDonald's for dinner?

W : Sorry. I have to get home. We're having company for dinner.

M : Oh? Who's coming?

W : My grandparents. I haven't seen them for a long time.

Question : Why won't the girl go to McDonald's for dinner?

A. She is going to eat at her grandparents' house.

B. She doesn't want to see her grandparents.

C. Her grandparents will visit her.

* company 〔'kʌmpənɪ 〕 *n.* 客人

grandparents 〔'grænd‚pɛrənts 〕 *n. pl.* 祖父母

visit 〔'vɪzɪt 〕 *v.* 拜訪

28. (**C**) W : It's time to sign up for a school club.

M : I know. Which one are you going to join?

W : Astronomy. I've always been interested in the stars.

M : That sounds interesting. I think I'll do the same.

Question : What does the boy mean?

A. He has also been interested in the stars for a long time.

B. He will look for a club that he has always been interested in.

C. He will join the Astronomy Club, too.

* ***sign up*** 報名加入 *< for >*   club 〔 klʌb 〕 *n.* 社團

astronomy 〔 ə'strɑnəmɪ 〕 *n.* 天文學

sound 〔 saʊnd 〕 *v.* 聽起來

interesting 〔'ɪntrɪstɪŋ 〕 *adj.* 有趣的   ***look for*** 尋找

29. (**C**) M : When is the next train to Kaohsiung?

W : At 3:20.

M : That's just five minutes from now. Two tickets, please, and hurry.

Question : What time did this conversation take place?

A. In the train station.

B. It departs at 3:20.

C. At a quarter after three.

* ***Kaohsiung*** 高雄　　***from now*** 離現在
hurry〔'hɝɪ〕v. 趕快
conversation〔͵kɑnvɚ'seʃən〕n. 對話
take place 發生　　depart〔dɪ'pɑrt〕v. 離開；出發
quarter〔'kwɔrtɚ〕n. 一刻鐘；十五分鐘
at a quarter after three 在三點十五分

30. (**A**) W : Do you have a pet?

M : I had a dog when I was in elementary school, but I don't have one now.

W : What happened to it?

M : It ran away.

Question : What happened to the boy's dog?

A. It got lost.

B. It was run over.

C. It lives in the elementary school.

* pet〔pɛt〕n. 寵物　　happen〔'hæpən〕v. 發生
run away 逃跑　　***get lost*** 走失　　***run over*** 輾過

二、閱讀能力測驗

第一部份：詞彙和結構

1. (**C**) The drunk driver is <u>responsible</u> for the serious accident.

這位酒醉的駕駛人應該為這場嚴重的車禍<u>負責</u>。

    (A) fluent〔'fluənt〕*adj.* 流利的 < *in* >

    (B) jealous〔'dʒɛləs〕*adj.* 嫉妒的 < *of* >

    (C) ***responsible***〔rɪ'spɑnsəbḷ〕*adj.* 應負責任的 < *for* >

    (D) greedy〔'gridɪ〕*adj.* 貪心的

    * drunk〔drʌŋk〕*adj.* 喝醉酒的

    driver〔'draɪvɚ〕*n.* 駕駛人

    serious〔'sɪrɪəs〕*adj.* 嚴重的

    accident〔'æksədənt〕*n.* 車禍

2. (**B**) The weather was so hot that the paper fan was not very <u>effective</u>.

天氣這麼熱，所以紙扇沒什麼<u>作用</u>。

    (A) changeable〔'tʃendʒəbḷ〕*adj.* 善變的

    (B) ***effective***〔ɪ'fɛktɪv〕*adj.* 有效的；起作用的

    (C) formal〔'fɔrmḷ〕*adj.* 正式的（ ↔ *informal* ）

    (D) funny〔'fʌnɪ〕*adj.* 好笑的；有趣的

    * weather〔'wɛðɚ〕*n.* 天氣

    so…that～ 如此…以致於～

    fan〔fæn〕*n.* 扇子　　***paper fan*** 紙扇

3. (**A**) Nancy hates all <u>bugs</u>, especially roaches.

南西討厭所有的<u>小蟲子</u>，特別是蟑螂。

(A) **bug**〔bʌg〕n. 小蟲子　　(B) bag〔bæg〕n. 袋子

(C) belt〔bɛlt〕n. 皮帶　　　(D) burger〔'bɝgɚ〕n. 漢堡

* hate〔het〕v. 討厭　　especially〔ə'spɛʃəlɪ〕adv. 特別是
roach〔rotʃ〕n. 蟑螂（= cockroach〔'kɑk,rotʃ〕）

4. (**D**) Cathy hid the candy in her right hand.　Then she held
out both hands and asked her brother to <u>guess</u> where
the candy was.

凱西把糖果藏在她的右手。然後她把雙手伸出來，要她哥哥
<u>猜</u>糖果在哪裡。

(A) raise〔rez〕v. 舉起　　(B) clap〔klæp〕v. 拍手

(C) shake〔ʃek〕v. 搖動　　(D) **guess**〔gɛs〕v. 猜測

* hide〔haɪd〕v. 隱藏（三態變化為：hide-hid-hidden）
candy〔'kændɪ〕n. 糖果　　right〔raɪt〕adj. 右邊的
hold out 伸出

5. (**A**) Today is my birthday, so my good friend will <u>treat</u> me
to a movie.

今天是我的生日，所以我的好朋友要<u>請</u>我去看電影。

(A) **treat**〔trit〕v. 請（客）　　　**treat** sb. **to** ~ 請某人 ~

(B) examine〔ɪg'zæmɪn〕v. 檢查

(C) reply〔rɪ'plaɪ〕v. 回答

(D) collect〔kə'lɛkt〕v. 收集

6. (**B**) Little Wendy cried loudly after bumping <u>into</u> the table.
小溫蒂在撞<u>到</u>桌子後，哭得很大聲。

　　bump into sth.　撞到某物

　* loudly〔'laʊdlɪ〕*adv.* 大聲地

7. (**B**) Carl worked at the bookstore last month, but he doesn't
work there <u>anymore</u>. 卡爾上個月在這家書店工作，但是
他現在已經不在那裡工作了。

　　not…anymore　不再…

　　而 (A) again〔ə'gɛn〕*adv.* 再一次，(C) anyway〔'ɛnɪ,we〕
adv. 無論如何，(D) anywhere〔'ɛnɪ,hwɛr〕*adv.* 任何地方，
皆不合句意。

　* bookstore〔'bʊk,stor〕*n.* 書店

8. (**C**) <u>Can</u> you go to the baseball game next Friday evening?
你下個星期五晚上<u>可以</u>去看棒球比賽嗎？

　　從 go 得知，空格須填助動詞 *Can*。而 (A) have 用於完
成式「have + p.p.」的形式，(B) are 用於未來式「are
going to」的形式，(D) did 須搭配表過去的時間副詞，
故用法皆不合。

9. (**D**) My parents do the housework during the week, but I
help <u>them</u> on the weekend.
我父母平日做家事，但我在週末的時候會幫<u>他們</u>。

　　空格填代替 my parents 的代名詞，用 *them*，選 (D)。

　* housework〔'haʊs,wɝk〕*n.* 家事
　　during〔'djʊrɪŋ〕*prep.* 在…期間
　　week〔wik〕*n.* 平日；工作日
　　weekend〔'wik'ɛnd〕*n.* 週末

10. (**A**)　We hurried into the building because it <u>was</u> raining
　　　　　　 harder and harder.
　　　　　　 我們匆忙進入這棟建築物，因爲外面的雨愈下愈大了。

　　　　　依句意，爲過去進行式，即「was/were + V-ing」的形式，
　　　　　it 爲單數主詞，故選 (A) ***was***。

　　　　 * hurry〔ˋhɝɪ〕v. 趕緊；匆忙
　　　　　 building〔ˋbɪldɪŋ〕n. 建築物　　 hard〔hɑrd〕adv. 猛烈地

11. (**B**)　I'm sorry.　I <u>can't</u> go to your birthday party next
　　　　　　 Wednesday.　對不起，我下星期三<u>無法</u>參加你的生日派對。

　　　　　從 I'm sorry. 可知，說話者無法參加，故選 (B) ***can't***。而
　　　　　(A) 可以，(C) 應該，(D) 不應該，均不合句意。

12. (**C**)　Most of the young girls <u>who</u> live in Taipei like to go
　　　　　　 shopping at the big department stores on holidays.
　　　　　　 大部分住在台北的年輕女孩，假日時喜歡去大型百貨公司
　　　　　　 購物。

　　　　　先行詞 young girls 爲人，故關係代名詞用 ***who***。

　　　　 * ***go shopping*** 去購物　　 ***department store*** 百貨公司
　　　　　 holiday〔ˋhɑləˌde〕n. 假日

13. (**C**)　Andy : Wow!　There are so many dolls in this shop!
　　　　　　 Patty : Yes, I like those red <u>ones</u>.　How about you?
　　　　　　 安迪：哇！這家店裡面有好多洋娃娃！
　　　　　　 佩蒂：是啊，我喜歡那些紅色的<u>洋娃娃</u>。那你呢？

　　　　　ones 代替先前提到的名詞 dolls。

　　　　 * doll〔dɑl〕n. 洋娃娃　　 shop〔ʃɑp〕n. 商店
　　　　　 How about you? 那你呢？(= ***What about you?***)

14. (**B**) Our team lost the game.　We played <u>badly</u> this time.

　　　我們這一隊輸了這場比賽。我們這一次打得很糟。

　　　　空格須填副詞，修飾動詞 played，故形容詞 (A) bad
　　　　「不好的」，(C) poor「差勁的」皆不合，而 (D) worst
　　　　爲 badly 的最高級，在此用法不合，故選 (B) *badly*
　　　　「糟糕地」。

　　　　* team〔tim〕*n.* 隊伍　　lose〔luz〕*v.* 輸掉（比賽）

15. (**C**) The first question is <u>easier</u> than the second question.

　　　第一個問題比第二個問題簡單。

　　　　由連接詞 than 可知，空格應填一比較級，easy 的比較級
　　　　是 *easier*，故選 (C)。

第二部份：段落填空

Questions 16-20

　　A doctor and an art teacher loved the same pretty woman

<u>who lived</u> in their apartment building.　One spring vacation, the
　16

teacher <u>was asked</u> to take his students to the country.　The night
　　　17

before he left, he gave the girl a <u>box</u> and told her, "I'll be away
　　　　　　　　　　　18

for a week.　I have a present for you.　Open it after I <u>leave</u>."
　　　　　　　　　　　　　　　19

When the girl opened it, she found seven apples and this <u>note</u>:
　　　　　　　　　　　　　　　　　20

"An apple a day keeps the doctor away."

　　有一個醫生與一個美術老師，同時愛上一個跟他們住在同一幢公寓的美麗女子。有一年春假，這位教師被要求必須帶學生去鄉下。在他要離開的前一晚，他給了這女孩一個盒子，然後對她說：「我要離開一個星期。我要給妳一個禮物。在我出門之後再打開。」當這女孩打開的時候，她發現有七顆蘋果跟這張紙條：「每天一顆蘋果，能讓妳不用看醫生。」

art〔ɑrt〕n. 美術　　same〔sem〕adj. 同一個
pretty〔ˋprɪtɪ〕adj. 漂亮的　　apartment〔əˋpɑrtmənt〕n. 公寓
building〔ˋbɪldɪŋ〕n. 建築物　　*spring vacation* 春假
country〔ˋkʌntrɪ〕n. 鄉下　　away〔əˋwe〕adv. 離開
present〔ˋprɛznt〕n. 禮物　　*keep~away* 使~遠離

16. (**B**) 先行詞 pretty woman 是人，故關係代名詞用 who 或 that，而形容詞子句中的動詞依句意為過去式，選 (B) *who lived*。

　　⎧ ⋯the same pretty woman *who lived* in⋯
　　⎩ = ⋯the same pretty woman *living* in⋯

17. (**D**) *ask* sb. + *to V.* 要求某人做~
這裡用被動語態，即「be 動詞 + p.p.」的形式，故選 (D) *was asked*。

18. (**D**) 依句意，這位女孩收到七個蘋果的禮物，應該是用「箱子」裝的，故選 (D) *box*。而 (A) toy「玩具」，(B) apple「蘋果」，(C) envelope〔ˋɛnvəˌlop〕n. 信封，均不合句意。

19. (**A**) 依句意，這是「表未來」的狀況，在 after 引導的副詞子句中，要用現在式代替未來式，故選 (A) *leave*。

20. (**D**) 依句意，選 (D) *note*〔not〕n. 字條。而 (A) 水果，(B) 答案，(C) 例子，均不合句意。

Questions 21-25

I bought my son a dog called Lassie last year. Dogs are children's friends. Mike had had no friends at <u>all</u> before Lassie

          21

<u>came</u>. Now, he enjoys <u>playing</u> with her every day. "Lassie is

22   23

cute and she is my best friend!" Mike is a happy boy now.

我去年買給我兒子一隻名叫萊西的狗。狗是小孩子的朋友。在萊希出現之前,麥克完全沒有朋友。現在他每天都很喜歡跟牠玩。「萊西很可愛,牠是我最好的朋友!」麥克現在是個快樂的小男孩。

      call 〔kɔl〕 *v.* 稱作   cute 〔kjut〕 *adj.* 可愛的

Mike can learn how to be kind to others. We <u>taught</u> him

                             24

how to get along with Lassie. He is now more polite to animals, and to other people!

麥克可以學會要如何體貼別人。我們敎他要如何跟萊西相處。他現在對動物更好,對人也更有禮貌!

      kind 〔kaɪnd〕 *adj.* 親切的   ***get along with*** 與~相處
      polite 〔pə'laɪt〕 *adj.* 有禮貌的   animal 〔'ænəml̩〕 *n.* 動物

Children love dogs and dogs love children. So why not

put them together and let them <u>have</u> a good time?

                          25

小孩喜歡狗,狗也喜歡小孩。所以為何不讓他們在一起,好好的玩呢?

21. (**B**) ***at all*** 一點也不 (用於否定句)

22. (**B**) 從過去完成式 had had 可知，空格動詞須用「過去式」，故
選 (B) *came*。

23. (**A**) *enjoy + V-ing* 喜歡～

24. (**A**) 依句意，我們「教」他如何與別人相處，選 (A) *taught*。

25. (**D**) 「*let* ＋ 受詞 ＋ 原形 *V.*」表「讓～…」。
have a good time 玩得愉快

第三部份：閱讀理解

Questions 26-28

根據這張火車時刻表回答問題。

火 車 時 刻 表

車站　出發 \ 火車車號	1001	1003	1009	1015
台北	06:06	07:00	08:40	13:05
台中	09:08	09:16	10:40	15:05
彰化	09:36	09:43	—	—
嘉義	10:46	10:27	11:43	—
台南	11:50	11:08	12:22	16:43
高雄	12:45	11:39	12:52	17:14

according to 根據　　schedule〔'skɛdʒul〕*n.* 時刻表
departure〔dɪ'partʃɚ〕*n.* 出發

26. (**D**) 從台北到高雄，哪一班火車最快？

(A) 1001 號班次。　　　　(B) 1003 號班次。

(C) 1009 號班次。　　　　(D) <u>1015 號班次。</u>

27. (**C**) 凱倫住在台北。她想去彰化探望她的祖父母。她不應該搭乘哪些火車？

(A) 1001 號和 1003 號班次。　(B) 1003 號和 1009 號班次。

(C) <u>1009 號和 1015 號班次。</u>　(D) 1003 號和 1015 號班次。

* "—" 表示該班火車沒有停靠此站。

28. (**A**) 哪些火車停靠最多站？

(A) <u>1001 號和 1003 號班次。</u>　(B) 1003 號和 1009 號班次。

(C) 1009 號和 1015 號班次。　(D) 1003 號和 1015 號班次。

* *make a stop* （火車）停靠（車站）

Questions 29-30

李安迪
現場演唱會

日　　期：二○○二年十二月二十日

時　　間：晚間八點到九點半

地　　點：台北市台大體育館

票　　價：新台幣五百元、九百元、一千兩百元

洽詢專線：0800-088-812

---

live〔laɪv〕*adj.* 現場的

concert〔'kɑnsɝt〕*n.* 演唱會

location〔lo'keʃən〕*n.* 地點

sports〔spɔrts〕*adj.* 運動的

center〔'sɛntɚ〕*n.* 中心　　price〔praɪs〕*n.* 價格

hotline〔'hɑt͵laɪn〕*n.* 熱線；洽詢專線

29. (**D**) 如果我們對演唱會有任何疑問的話，可以怎麼辦？

    (A) 寄信。

    (B) 寄電子郵件。

    (C) 傳真。

    (D) 打電話。

    * send〔sɛnd〕*v.* 寄；傳　　letter〔'lɛtɚ〕*n.* 信

    e-mail〔'i͵mel〕*n.* 電子郵件　　fax〔fæks〕*n.* 傳真

    make a phone call 打電話

30. (**D**) 下列何者正確？

(A) 李安迪將在台北舉行兩場演唱會。

(B) 有四種不同的票。

(C) 這場演唱會將持續兩個小時。

(D) <u>這場演唱會將在十二月舉行。</u>

* following〔'faləwɪŋ〕*adj.* 下列的

true〔tru〕*adj.* 真實的；正確的

kind〔kaɪnd〕*n.* 種類

last〔læst〕*v.* 持續

hold〔hold〕*v.* 舉行

Questions 31-33

Mr. Lee is a farmer. He works on his farm every day. It is very hot on the farm. So when he takes a rest, he usually sits under a tree because it is cooler there.

李先生是個農夫。他每天都在田裡工作。田裡非常的熱。所以當他休息的時候，他通常會坐在樹下，因為那兒比較涼爽。

farmer〔'farmɚ〕n. 農夫　　farm〔farm〕n. 農田
take a rest 休息　　cool〔kul〕adj. 涼爽的

A few days ago, Mr. Lee saw a rabbit. The rabbit was running very fast. Then it hit a tree and died. Mr. Lee was very happy because he had a rabbit. He thought, "Soon I'll have a lot more rabbits. I'll sell them in the market. Soon I'll have a lot of money. I'll never have to work hard in the field anymore." He decided to sit under the tree to wait for more rabbits.

幾天前，李先生看到一隻兔子。那隻兔子跑得很快，然後牠撞到樹，之後就死了。李先生非常高興，因為他抓到了一隻兔子。他想：「我很快就會有很多兔子，到時候我可以拿去市場賣。沒多久我就發財了。我就永遠不用辛苦種田了。」他決定要坐在樹下等待更多的兔子。

rabbit〔'ræbɪt〕n. 兔子　　hit〔hɪt〕v. 撞到（三態同形）
die〔daɪ〕v. 死亡　　market〔'markɪt〕n. 市場
hard〔hard〕adv. 努力地；辛苦地　　field〔fild〕n. 田野
decide〔dɪ'saɪd〕v. 決定　　**wait for** 等待

He has sat under the tree for more than one week, but no rabbits have hit the tree. He doesn't know that the same thing will not happen if he just sits and waits.

他坐在樹下超過一個禮拜了，但卻沒有半隻兔子撞到樹。他並不知道，如果他只是坐著等的話，同樣的事是不會再發生的。

31. (**C**) 這隻兔子是怎麼死的？

    (A) 牠被這名農夫殺死。

    (B) 牠被一位獵人殺死。

    (C) <u>牠跑太快，所以撞到樹之後，就死掉了。</u>

    (D) 天氣太炎熱，所以牠就死掉了。

    * kill〔kɪl〕*v.* 殺死   hunter〔'hʌntɚ〕*n.* 獵人

    so…that～ 如此…以致於～

32. (**C**) 農夫爲什麼想要兔子？

    (A) 他想要自己一個人把牠們吃掉。

    (B) 他想要跟家人一起把牠們吃掉。

    (C) <u>他想要把牠們賣掉賺錢。</u>

    (D) 他想要把牠們送給朋友。

    * *What～for?* 爲什麼～？（＝*Why～?*）

    all by oneself 獨自   family〔'fæməlɪ〕*n.* 家人

33. (**D**) 這個故事的啓示爲何？

    (A) 兔子很愚蠢。

    (B) 人如果夠幸運，就不需要辛苦工作。

    (C) 兔子的運氣不好。

    (D) <u>懶惰的人很愚蠢。</u>

    * lesson〔'lɛsn̩〕*n.* 教訓；啓示   story〔'storɪ〕*n.* 故事

    stupid〔'stjupɪd〕*adj.* 愚蠢的   lucky〔'lʌkɪ〕*adj.* 幸運的

    lazy〔'lezɪ〕*adj.* 懶惰的

Questions 34-35

August 16, 2002

Dear Ms. Huang,

　　I'm writing this letter to you because my son, Frank Wu, who is in your class, cannot go to school today.

　　This morning, when he woke up, he did not feel very well. We went to see a doctor and he was given some medicine. The doctor said that he had to stay at home for one or two days. My wife and I will let him go back to school when he feels better.

　　Thank you very much.

　　　　　　　　　　　　　　　　　Yours truly,
　　　　　　　　　　　　　　　　　Tony Wu

　　　　　　　　　　　　　　二〇〇二年八月十六日

親愛的黃老師：

　　我會寫這封信給妳，是因為我兒子法蘭克吳，他是你班上的學生，今天沒辦法上學。

　　他今天早上起床的時候，就覺得不太舒服。我帶他去看醫生，拿了一些藥。醫生說他必須在家休息一兩天。等他覺得好一點之後，我跟我太太會讓他回到學校的。

　　非常感謝妳。

　　　　　　　　　　　　　　　　吳東尼　敬上

Ms.〔mɪz〕*n.* 女士　　***wake up*** 醒來

well〔wɛl〕*adj.* 身體健康的　　medicine〔'mɛdəsn̩〕*n.* 藥

stay〔ste〕*v.* 停留；留下　　***go back to*** 回到

yours truly 敬上（用於書信結尾）

34. (**B**)　為什麼法蘭克不能上學？

　　　　(A) 他媽媽生病了。　　　　(B) 他生病了。

　　　　(C) 他很晚才起床。　　　　(D) 他很懶惰。

　　　　* late〔let〕*adv.* 晚

35. (**B**)　誰是黃女士？

　　　　(A) 法蘭克的醫生。　　　　(B) 法蘭克的老師。

　　　　(C) 法蘭克的媽媽。　　　　(D) 吳東尼的老師。

三、寫作能力測驗

第一部份：單句寫作

第 1~5 題：句子改寫

1. Two boys are playing badminton at the playground.

　Who ＿＿＿＿＿＿＿＿＿＿＿＿＿＿＿＿＿＿＿＿＿＿＿＿？

　　重點結構：wh-問句的用法

　　　解　答：Who is playing badminton at the playground?

　　句型分析：Who + be 動詞 + 現在分詞？

　　　說　明：Who 做主詞時，須視為單數，故 be 動詞用 is。

　　* badminton〔'bædmɪntən〕*n.* 羽毛球

　　playground〔'ple͵graʊnd〕*n.*（學校的）操場

2. Eating too much is bad for your health.

It is _____.

> 重點結構：以 It 為虛主詞引導的句子
>
> 解　答：It is bad for your health to eat too much.
>
> 句型分析：It is ＋ 形容詞 ＋ 不定詞
>
> 說　明：虛主詞 It 代替不定詞片語，不定詞片語則置於句
> 　　　　尾，故 eating too much 改為 to eat too much。
>
> * health〔hεlθ〕 n. 健康

3. I eat and sleep a lot.

_____ last weekend.

> 重點結構：過去式動詞
>
> 解　答：I ate and slept a lot last weekend.
>
> 句型分析：主詞 ＋ 動詞
>
> 說　明：由時間副詞 last weekend 可知，動詞須用過去
> 　　　　式，eat 和 sleep 是不規則動詞，其過去式是 ate
> 　　　　和 slept。

4. My parents bought some comic books for me.

My parents _____ comic books.

> 重點結構：buy 的用法
>
> 解　答：My parents bought me some comic books.
>
> 句型分析：buy ＋ 間接受詞（人）＋ 直接受詞（物）
>
> 說　明：「買東西給某人」有兩種寫法：「buy ＋ *sth.* ＋ for
> 　　　　＋ *sb.*」或「buy ＋ *sb.* ＋ *sth.*」，這題要改成第二種
> 　　　　用法，先寫人（me），再寫物（comic books）。
>
> * *comic book* 漫畫書

5. "I like your new shoes," I said to Mary.
   I said to Mary that _____.

　　重點結構：直接引用改為間接引用的用法

　　　解　答：<u>I said to Mary that I liked her new shoes.</u>

　　句型分析：I said to Mary + that + 主詞 + 動詞

　　　說　明：" "裡面的話是直接引用，若去掉" "，則是間接引
　　　　　　　用的用法，即 that 引導的名詞子句，做為動詞 said
　　　　　　　的受詞，子句中的動詞要和主要動詞 said 的時態相
　　　　　　　同，所以 like 須改成 liked，而所有格 your 是指
　　　　　　　「瑪麗的」，故在間接引用時，改成 her。

　　* shoes〔ʃuz〕*n. pl.* 鞋子

第 6～10 題：句子合併

6. Polly can't speak Japanese.
   Rita can't speak Japanese.
   Neither _____.

　　重點結構：「neither…nor～」的用法

　　　解　答：<u>Neither Polly nor Rita can speak Japanese.</u>

　　句型分析：Neither + A + nor + B + 助動詞 + 動詞

　　　說　明：這題是說波莉不會說日文，莉塔也不會說日文，所
　　　　　　　以兩個人都不會說日文，用「neither…nor～」來
　　　　　　　連接兩個主詞，表「兩者皆不」。

　　* Japanese〔͵dʒæpə'niz〕*n.* 日語

7. Kevin is very young.

Kevin cannot go to school.

Kevin is too _____.

重點結構：「too + 形容詞 + to V.」的用法

解　答：<u>Kevin is too young to go to school.</u>

句型分析：主詞 + be 動詞 + too + 形容詞 + to V.

説　明：這題的意思是說「凱文年紀太小，沒辦法上學」，用 too…to V. 合併，表「太…以致於不～」。

8. I have a sister.

My sister's name is Jennifer.

I have _____ Jennifer.

重點結構：whose 的用法

解　答：<u>I have a sister whose name is Jennifer.</u>

句型分析：I have a sister + whose + 名詞 + 動詞

説　明：這題的意思是說「我有一個名叫珍妮佛的姊姊」，在合併時，用 whose 表示所有格，引導形容詞子句。

9. I like to eat peanut butter very much.

My brother doesn't like to eat peanut butter.

I like _____ peanut butter very much, _____ it.

重點結構：but 的用法

解　答：<u>I like to eat peanut butter very much, but my brother doesn't like it.</u>

句型分析：主詞 + 動詞 + but + 主詞 + 動詞

説　明：but 是對等連接詞，表示語氣上的轉折。

* ***peanut butter*** 花生醬

10. Bob is fixing his computer.

Nancy helps him.

Nancy helps _____.

重點結構：「help + *sb.* + (to) V.」的用法

解　答：<u>Nancy helps Bob (to) fix his computer.</u>

句型分析：help + 受詞 + 不定詞或原形動詞

説　明：這題的意思是「南西幫巴伯修電腦」，help 的用法
是接受詞後，須接不定詞，不定詞的 to 也可省略。

＊ fix〔fɪks〕*v.* 修理　　computer〔kəmˋpjutɚ〕*n.* 電腦

第 11～15 題：重組

11. What _____?

Kelly / her / do / like / animals / and / mother

重點結構：「What + 複數名詞？」的用法

解　答：<u>What animals do Kelly and her mother like?</u>

句型分析：What + 複數名詞 + 助動詞 + 主詞 + 動詞？

説　明：這題的意思是「凱莉和她媽媽喜歡什麼動物？」

12. I _____.

at all / orange / don't / juice / like

重點結構：「not…at all」的用法

解　答：<u>I don't like orange juice at all.</u>

句型分析：主詞 + 助動詞的否定 + 動詞 + 受詞 + at all

説　明：這題的意思是「我一點都不喜歡柳橙」，not…at all
表示「一點也不」，為否定句的加強語氣。

＊ juice〔dʒus〕*n.* 果汁

13. David _____.
   best / is / one / friends / my / of

   重點結構：「one of + 所有格 + 複數名詞」的用法

   解　答：<u>David is one of my best friends.</u>

   句型分析：主詞 + be 動詞 + one of + 所有格 + 複數名詞

   説　明：題目的意思是「大衛是我最好的朋友之一」，「～當中的一個」用「one of + 複數名詞」來表示。

14. Sandra _____.
   earthquake / when / watching / the / happened / was / TV

   重點結構：「主詞 + 動詞 + when 子句」的用法

   解　答：<u>Sandra was watching TV when the earthquake happened.</u>

   句型分析：主詞 + be 動詞 + 現在分詞 + when + 主詞 + 動詞

   説　明：地震（earthquake）和發生（happened）連在一起，看（watching）和電視（TV）放在一起，重組成此句「當地震發生時，珊卓拉正在看電視」。

   * earthquake〔'ɜθ,kwek〕n. 地震

15. Please _____.
   page / turn to / seven / number

   重點結構：祈使句的用法

   解　答：<u>Please turn to page number seven.</u>

   句型分析：Please + 原形動詞

   説　明：這題的意思是「請翻到第七頁」，用祈使句的句型，須以原形動詞開頭。

   * turn〔tɜn〕v. 翻動　　page〔pedʒ〕n. 頁

第二部份：段落寫作

題目： 上星期天，我們全家出遊到山上野餐（have a picnic），請
　　　根據圖片內容寫一篇約 50 字的簡短描述。

　　Last Sunday, my family and I drove to the mountains. We
had a picnic beside a lake. My father tried to catch some fish in
the lake. My mother and I cooked some food on a barbecue. My
little brother and sister played with a ball. *Later on* we all ate the
food. We had a good time *last Sunday*.

drive〔draɪv〕v. 開車　　mountain〔'maʊntn̩〕n. 山
picnic〔'pɪknɪk〕n. 野餐　　*have a picnic* 去野餐
beside〔bɪ'saɪd〕prep. 在…旁邊　　lake〔lek〕n. 湖
try to + V. 試著要～　　catch〔kætʃ〕v. 捕捉
cook〔kʊk〕v. 烹煮　　barbecue〔'bɑrbɪˌkju〕n. 烤肉架
play with 玩～　　*later on* 之後（= *later*）

心得筆記欄

全民英語能力分級檢定測驗
初級測驗 ④

一、聽力測驗

本測驗分三部份，全為三選一之選擇題，每部份各 10 題，共 30 題，作答時間約 20 分鐘。

第一部份：看圖辨義

本部份共 10 題，試題冊上每題有一個圖片，請聽錄音機播出一個相關的問題，與 A、B、C 三個英語敘述後，選一個與所看到圖片最相符的答案，並在答案紙上相對的圓圈內塗黑作答。每題播出一遍，問題及選項均不印在試題冊上。

例：（看）

NT$80 NT$50

（聽）

Look at the picture. How much is the hamburger?

A. It's eighty dollars.
B. It's fifty-five dollars.
C. It's eighteen dollars.

正確答案為 A

Question 1

Question 2

Question 3

Question 4

Question 5

Question 6

請 翻 頁 ▌▏⟹

Question 7

Question 8

Question 9

Question 10

請翻頁 ⟹

第二部份：問答

本部份共 10 題，每題錄音機會播出一個問句或直述句，
每題播出一次，聽後請從試題冊上 A、B、C 三個選項中，
選出一個最適合的回答或回應，並在答案紙上塗黑作答。

例：

（聽）Good morning, Kevin. How are you?

（看）A. I'm fine, thank you.
　　　B. I'm in the living room.
　　　C. My name is Kevin.

正確答案為 A

11. A. It leaves at 8:00.
　　B. Not until 7:30.
　　C. It's at the stadium.

12. A. It will start at 8 p.m.
　　B. Please come in.
　　C. I'm glad you could come.

13. A. May fifteenth.
　　B. I'm fifteen.
　　C. 1988.

14. A. Yes, it's my favorite sport.
　　B. Yes, and Michael Jordan is my favorite player.
　　C. No, I'm not on the team.

15. A. Was anyone hurt?
    B. Is that why you are
       late?
    C. That must have been
       very frightening.

16. A. You can take a bus,
       but the MRT is faster.
    B. You can get there in
       10 minutes.
    C. It's on the west side
       of town.

17. A. I went shopping.
    B. I usually do my
       homework after
       dinner.
    C. I want to see a movie.

18. A. It's on the second
       floor.
    B. It's very difficult.
    C. It's at 3:00.

19. A. It was two weeks
       long.
    B. I went to visit my
       grandparents.
    C. It was great.

20. A. All right. I'll get my
       bike.
    B. It's too far to walk.
    C. I'd rather not. It's
       going to rain.

請 翻 頁 ⟩

第三部份： 簡短對話

　　本部份共 10 題，每題錄音機會播出一段對話及一個相關的問題，每題播出兩次，聽後請從試題冊上 A、B、C 三個選項中，選出一個最適合的回答，並在答案紙上塗黑作答。

　　例：

（聽）(Woman) Good afternoon, ...Mr. Davis?

　　　 (Man) 　　Yes. I have an appointment with Dr. Sanders at two o'clock. My son Tommy has a fever.

　　　 (Woman) Oh, that's too bad. Well, please have a seat, Mr. Davis. Dr. Sanders will be right with you.

　　　 Question: Where did this conversation take place?

（看）A. In a post office.

　　　 B. In a restaurant.

　　　 C. In a doctor's office.

　　　　　正確答案為 C

21. A. He gets to school by
    MRT.
   B. The MRT is cheaper
    than the bus.
   C. The bus is slower
    than the MRT.

22. A. He has trouble
    leaving at seven
    o'clock.
   B. He is often late for
    school.
   C. School starts at
    seven o'clock.

23. A. He gave her 15
    dollars.
   B. He changed her
    small fries into a
    medium.
   C. He gave her a tip.

24. A. He is too young to
    carry the cake.
   B. There are four
    children in his family.
   C. He has no brothers or
    sisters.

25. A. He wants to copy the
    girl's homework.
   B. He wants to watch
    the game.
   C. He wants to look at
    the sports page.

26. A. The girl should run or
    she will be late for
    class.
   B. The time shown on
    the clock is not correct.
   C. The clock should
    speed up.

請 翻 頁 ⇒

27. A. He was at the
       library.
    B. He was making a
       telephone call.
    C. He was doing
       homework.

28. A. In an airplane.
    B. In a train station.
    C. On a bus.

29. A. He always drinks tea
       in the morning.
    B. He wants to do
       something different.
    C. There is no more
       coffee.

30. A. He will study right
       before the test.
    B. He will only study
       for one minute.
    C. The test will start in
       one minute.

二、閱讀能力測驗

　　本測驗分三部份，全為四選一之選擇題，共 35 題，作答時間 35 分鐘。

第一部份：詞彙和結構

　　　　　　本部份共 15 題，每題含一個空格。請就試題冊上 A、B、C、D 四個選項中選出最適合題意的字或詞，標示在答案紙上。

1. Remember to close both the doors and the _____ before you leave the classroom.
   A. lights
   B. windows
   C. computers
   D. fans

2. When Mr. Lin is not home, there are usually several messages on the answering _____.
   A. machine
   B. telephone
   C. door
   D. card

3. After taking a bath, dry your body with a clean _____.
   A. towel
   B. tissue
   C. toothbrush
   D. toothpaste

請 翻 頁 ⫸

4. If you think the bus is going too fast, you may tell the
   _____ to slow down.
   A. teacher
   B. singer
   C. driver
   D. clerk

5. Sending _____ is faster than writing a letter. More and
   more people are using it to write to their friends.
   A. pen
   B. finger
   C. communication
   D. e-mail

6. Thank goodness the exams are _____. We can relax now!
   A. out
   B. with
   C. down
   D. over

7. Be patient with your brother. _____, he is only three
   years old.
   A. At last
   B. After all
   C. At first
   D. All the time

8. The doctor told me _____ the medicine three times a day.
   A. taking
   B. to take
   C. to taking
   D. take

9. _____ May and Edward told you the good news that we won the basketball game?
   A. Have
   B. Has
   C. Did
   D. Do

10. _____ the radio and listen to the "English Garden" program.
   A. Turning on
   B. To turn on
   C. Turn on
   D. Turned on

11. Did you notice Mother _____ a new dress?
   A. wear
   B. worn
   C. to wear
   D. wore

請 翻 頁 ⟹

12. Mr. Wu makes much money _____ writing storybooks.

    A. about

    B. by

    C. to

    D. with

13. Paul often practices _____ English with the CD.

    A. speaking

    B. to speak

    C. to speaking

    D. spoken

14. George slipped on the floor, but he didn't hurt _____.

    A. him

    B. her

    C. himself

    D. herself

15. Tom hates studying history. He has no interest in learning foreign languages _____.

    A. either

    B. neither

    C. besides

    D. too

第二部份：段落填空

本部份共 10 題，包括二個段落，每個段落各含 5 個空格。
請就試題冊上 A、B、C、D 四個選項中選出最適合題意
的字或詞，標示在答案紙上。

Questions 16-20

Many junior high students have started to look ___(16)___ their ideal boyfriends or girlfriends. Our teacher said it was not the right time. She asked us to think about ___(17)___ we come to school. "Studying is your most important job here," she said. "Also, you may be too young ___(18)___ some problems."

Then I asked my ___(19)___ brother, David, about this. He said, "Three years ago, I fell in love with a girl. I spent most of my time ___(20)___ out with her. My grades became worse, but my girlfriend still did well in her studies. So, it depends, I think."

16. A. for
    B. into
    C. out
    D. in

17. A. when
    B. where
    C. why
    D. how

18. A. and solve
    B. to solve
    C. for solving
    D. to solving

19. A. seventeen-years-old
    B. seventeenth-year-old
    C. seventeen-year-olds
    D. seventeen-year-old

20. A. go
    B. going
    C. to go
    D. to going

請 翻 頁 ◁▭▭⟹

Questions 21-25

Dear Steve,

I was pleased to get your letter. It reminds me of the happy days we ___(21)___ together. As you know, I love nature. Last week, I ___(22)___ with my family to Yangmingshan National Park. I saw many flowers there. The air ___(23)___ the singing of birds and the wonderful smell of flowers. Along with this letter is a photo ___(24)___ in front of a beautiful scenic spot. I'm sure ___(25)___ you'll agree it is very beautiful.

Remember me to your family.

With love,
Linda

21. A. spent
    B. took
    C. cost
    D. started

22. A. went a trip
    B. took a trip
    C. took on a trip
    D. took up a trip

23. A. was full with
    B. was full of
    C. were full with
    D. were full of

24. A. took
    B. take
    C. taken
    D. to taken

25. A. of
    B. about
    C. which
    D. that

第三部份： 閱讀理解

本部份共 10 題，包括數段短文，每段短文後有 1～3 個相
關問題，請就試題冊上 A、B、C、D 四個選項中選出最
適合者，標示在答案紙上。

Questions 26-27

ALOHA BEACH

A Great Place to enjoy sunshine!

Rules:
1. No boating.
2. No fishing.
3. No fires.
4. Swimming hours: 8 am — 8 pm
5. Volleyball hours: 2 pm — 5 pm

26. What can you do at Aloha Beach?
   A. Go boating.   B. Start a fire for a barbecue.
   C. Play with water.   D. Fish.

27. If you get to Aloha Beach at 6 o'clock in the evening, can
you swim and play volleyball?
   A. You cannot do either.
   B. You can swim, but you cannot play volleyball.
   C. You can play volleyball, but you cannot swim.
   D. We don't know.

請翻頁

Questions 28-29

FAST FOOD EXPRESS

FOOD	PRICE ($NT)	DRINKS	PRICE ($NT)
Hot Dog	30	Iced Lemon Tea	25
Cheeseburger	25	Coke / Sprite / Fanta	20
Beef Sandwich	40	Hot Coffee	25
Fries	35	Mineral Water	15
Chicken Drumstick	40		
Fruit Salad	50		

28. Which food and drink together are most expensive?
    A. Fries and Coke.
    B. Beef sandwich and Sprite.
    C. Cheeseburger and iced lemon tea.
    D. Fruit salad and mineral water.

29. Helen does not eat meat. What can she buy?
    A. Hot dog.
    B. Drumstick.
    C. Beef sandwich.
    D. Fruit salad.

Questions 30-31

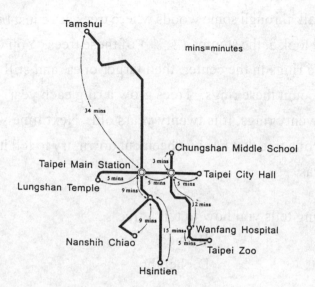

30. The Young family are going to Taipei Zoo to see koalas and penguins. They will take the MRT from Taipei City Hall station. How long will it take to get to Taipei Zoo?
    A. At least 22 minutes.
    B. At least 17 minutes.
    C. At least 12 minutes.
    D. At least 10 minutes.

31. Helen wants to go to Tamshui with her family. It would take them about 39 minutes to get there. Where are they now?
    A. Chungshan Middle School.
    B. Lungshan Temple.
    C. Taipei City Hall.
    D. Taipei Main Station.

請 翻 頁 ◖⟹

Questions 32-34

Take a walk through some woods where trees have just been cut down, and look at the stumps（殘株）of these trees. You will see many little rings in the center, then larger ones, and still larger ones. Count these rings. Trees grow a ring each year. So if a tree has twenty rings, it is twenty years old. Next time you see the stump of a tree that has just been cut down, try to tell how old the tree was.

32. This reading tells you how to tell a tree's
    A. age.   B. size.
    C. weight.   D. height.

33. A tree's age is learned by looking at the tree's
    A. leaves.   B. bark.
    C. roots.   D. stump.

34. What is true?
    A. A tree with seven rings has been growing for seven years.
    B. A twenty-year-old tree has more than twenty rings.
    C. The number of rings a tree has is decided by how much water the tree has got.
    D. Different kinds of trees have different kinds of ways to show how old they are.

Question 35

NO VISITORS
MAY ENTER
WITHOUT A TICKET

35. What does this sign mean?

A. People who want to enter need to hold a ticket.

B. People who want to visit enter the ticket office.

C. People who want to buy a ticket enter this door.

D. People who visit may get a parking ticket from
the police.

請 翻 頁

三、寫作能力測驗

　　本測驗共有兩部份，第一部份為單句寫作，第二部份為段落寫作。測驗時間為 40 分鐘。

第一部份：單句寫作

　　　　　　請將答案寫在寫作能力測驗答案紙對應的題號旁，如有拼字、標點、大小寫之錯誤，將予扣分。

第 1~5 題：句子改寫

　　　　　　請依題目之提示，將原句改寫成指定型式，並將改寫的句子完整地寫在答案紙上（包括提示之文字及標點符號）。

1. My boyfriend cooked me some spaghetti.

   My boyfriend _____ me.

2. Cartoons are interesting to most children.

   Most children are _____ cartoons.

3. Tina went to the swimming school.

   When _____?

4. To keep it a secret may be a good idea.

   It _____.

5. The Greens bought that house last week.

   That house _____ last week.

第 6～10 題：句子合併

　　　　請依照題目指示，將兩句合併成一句，並將合併的句子
　　　　完整地寫在答案紙上（包括提示之文字及標點符號）。

6. I saw my brother in the living room.
   My brother was watching TV.

   I saw _____ in the living room.

7. This postcard is pretty.
   That postcard is pretty.

   This postcard _____ as that postcard.

8. We have to walk fast.
   We want to catch the train.

   Walk fast, or _____ will not _____.

9. I have been reading a novel.
   I just finished it two days ago.

   I just finished _____.

10. My dog is smart.
    My dog is cute.

    My dog is not only _____.

請 翻 頁 ⫸

第 11～15 題：重組

請將題目中所有提示字詞整合成一有意義的句子，並將重組的句子完整地寫在答案紙上（包括提示之文字及標點符號）。答案中必須使用所有提示字詞，且不能隨意增加字詞，否則不予計分。

11. Do you know _____?
    when / plane / take / the / off / will

12. Which _____, black or white?
    like / color / you / better / do

13. It's _____.
    impossible / near / to find / a / almost / parking space
    / our school

14. How _____?
    you / would / your / like / steak

15. Robert _____.
    come / this evening / will / to / visit / us

第二部份: 段落寫作

題目: 昨天是中秋節 (Mid-Autumn Festival) ，請根據圖片內容寫一
　　　篇約 50 字的簡短描述。

初級英檢模擬試題④詳解

一、聽力測驗

第一部份

Look at the picture for question 1.

1. (**B**) What is on the desk?
   A. She is on the Internet.
   B. There are three pencils.
   C. She likes to drink coffee.

   * Internet〔'ɪntɚ,nɛt〕 *n.* 網際網路
     coffee〔'kɔfɪ〕 *n.* 咖啡

Look at the picture for question 2.

2. (**A**) How many people are driving on the street?
   A. There are two drivers on the street.
   B. There are seven cars on the street.
   C. They are parking the cars.

   * drive〔draɪv〕 *v.* 開車
     street〔strit〕 *n.* 街道
     driver〔'draɪvɚ〕 *n.* 駕駛人
     park〔pɑrk〕 *v.* 停（車）

Look at the picture for question 3.

3. (**C**) What are they going to do?
   A. They are going to sing a song.
   B. They are waiting for a bus.
   C. They are going to have their picture taken.

   * ***wait for*** 等待
     have *one's* ***picture taken*** 照相

Look at the picture for question 4.

4. (**B**) Where is the cat?
   A. The cat is climbing.
   B. It is on the roof.
   C. It is above the house.

   * climb〔klaɪm〕*v.* 爬　　roof〔ruf〕*n.* 屋頂
     above〔ə'bʌv〕*prep.* 在…上方
     注意：(B) 選項表示貓和屋頂有接觸；(C) 選項表示貓在屋頂
     　　　上方，但沒有碰觸到屋頂。

Look at the picture for question 5.

5. (**B**) What does she want?
   A. She wants an apple.
   B. She wants to lose weight.
   C. She wants a new dress.

   * ***lose weight*** 減重
     dress〔drɛs〕*n.* 洋裝

Look at the picture for question 6.

6. (**B**) What is the boy doing?

    A. He is bored.

    B. He is sleeping.

    C. He is writing the alphabet.

    * bored〔bord〕*adj.* 感到無聊的

     sleep〔slip〕*v.* 睡覺

     alphabet〔'ælfə,bɛt〕*n.* 字母（表）

Look at the picture for question 7.

7. (**C**) What is the giraffe doing?

    A. She is pointing at it.

    B. The giraffe is inside the cage.

    C. It is eating.

    * giraffe〔dʒə'ræf〕*n.* 長頸鹿

     point〔pɔɪnt〕*v.* 指著 <*at*>

     inside〔ɪn'saɪd〕*prep.* 在…裡面

     cage〔kedʒ〕*n.* 籠子

Look at the picture for question 8.

8. (**A**) What does the woman like to do in the park?

    A. She likes to walk her dog.

    B. She likes her dog.

    C. She wants to find her dog.

    * walk〔wɔk〕*v.* 遛（狗）

Look at the picture for question 9.

9. (**B**) What can't you do when you see this?

       A. Drink.

       B. Use water.

       C. Go swimming.

       * drink〔drɪŋk〕v. 喝酒   use〔juz〕v. 使用
       swim〔swɪm〕v. 游泳

Look at the picture for question 10.

10. (**A**) Why is the baby crying?

       A. He is hungry.

       B. He is crying very loudly.

       C. He cannot reach the ball.

       * cry〔kraɪ〕v. 哭   hungry〔'hʌŋgrɪ〕adj. 飢餓的
       loudly〔'laʊdlɪ〕adv. 大聲地
       reach〔ritʃ〕v. 伸手拿到

第二部份

11. (**B**) What time does the concert start?

       A. It leaves at 8:00.

       B. Not until 7:30.

       C. It's at the stadium.

       * concert〔'kɑnsɝt〕n. 音樂會；演唱會
       start〔start〕v. 開始   leave〔liv〕v. 離開
       not until ~ 直到~（才…）
       stadium〔'stedɪəm〕n. 體育場

12. (**C**) It was a wonderful party.

        A. It will start at 8 p.m.

        B. Please come in.

        C. I'm glad you could come.

        * wonderful (ˈwʌndəfəl) *adj.* 很棒的
          glad (glæd) *adj.* 高興的

13. (**A**) When is your birthday?

        A. May fifteenth.   B. I'm fifteen.

        C. 1988.

14. (**A**) Are you a baseball fan?

        A. Yes, it's my favorite sport.

        B. Yes, and Michael Jordan is my favorite player.

        C. No, I'm not on the team.

        * baseball (ˈbes,bɔl) *n.* 棒球   fan (fæn) *n.* 迷
          favorite (ˈfevərɪt) *adj.* 最喜愛的   sport (sport) *n.* 運動
          player (ˈpleə) *n.* 球員   team (tim) *n.* 隊

15. (**B**) My alarm didn't go off this morning.

        A. Was anyone hurt?

        B. Is that why you are late?

        C. That must have been very frightening.

        * alarm (əˈlɑrm) *n.* 鬧鐘 (= *alarm clock*)
          go off (鬧鐘)響   hurt (hɝt) *v.* 使受傷
          late (let) *adj.* 遲到的   ***must have been*** + *p.p.* 當時一定
          frightening (ˈfraɪtn̩ɪŋ) *adj.* 可怕的

16. (**A**) What is the best way to get to the train station?

  A. You can take a bus, but the MRT is faster.

  B. You can get there in 10 minutes.

  C. It's on the west side of town.

  * ***get to*** 到達 ***MRT*** 捷運 west〔wɛst〕*adj.* 西方的

   west side 西邊 town〔taʊn〕*n.* 市區

17. (**A**) What did you do last night?

  A. I went shopping.

  B. I usually do my homework after dinner.

  C. I want to see a movie.

  * ***see a movie*** 看電影

18. (**C**) When is your English class?

  A. It's on the second floor.

  B. It's very difficult.

  C. It's at 3:00.

  * floor〔flor〕*n.* 樓層 difficult〔'dɪfəˌkʌlt〕*adj.* 困難的

19. (**C**) How was your vacation?

  A. It was two weeks long.

  B. I went to visit my grandparents.

  C. It was great.

  * vacation〔ve'keʃən〕*n.* 假期

   visit〔'vɪzɪt〕*v.* 拜訪；探望

   grandparents〔'grændˌpɛrənts〕*n. pl.* 祖父母

   great〔gret〕*adj.* 很棒的

20. (**C**) Let's go for a walk.
  A. All right. I'll get my bike.
  B. It's too far to walk.
  C. I'd rather not. It's going to rain.

* *go for a walk* 去散步（= *take a walk*）
  All right. 好。　　get〔gɛt〕*v.* 取；拿來
  bike〔baɪk〕*n.* 腳踏車（= *bicycle*）
  too…to V. 太…，以致於不～
  far〔fɑr〕*adj.* 遙遠的
  would rather 寧願

第三部份

21. (**C**) W：How did you get to school today?
  M：I took the MRT as usual.
  W：But isn't it cheaper to take a bus?
  M：A little. But the MRT is a lot faster.

  Question：Why does the boy take the MRT to school?

  A. He gets to school by MRT.
  B. The MRT is cheaper than the bus.
  C. The bus is slower than the MRT.

* *as usual* 像往常一樣
  a little 一點點
  a lot 許多（修飾比較級，加強語氣）
  slow〔slo〕*adj.* 慢的

22. (**B**) W : What time do you leave for school?

M : About seven o'clock.

W : Isn't it hard to get to school on time when you leave so late?

M : Yes, I'm often in trouble for that.

Question : What does the boy mean?

A. He has trouble leaving at seven o'clock.

B. He is often late for school.

C. School starts at seven o'clock.

* **leave for** 動身前往　　hard〔hɑrd〕*adj.* 困難的

on time 準時　　late〔let〕*adv.* 晚　*adj.* 遲到的

be in trouble 有問題；有困難

have trouble + **V-ing** 做～有困難

school〔skul〕*n.* 上課

23. (**A**) W : I'd like a burger, small fries and medium orange juice.

M : That will be 85 dollars.

W : Here's one hundred.

M : Thank you.　Here's your change.

Question : What did the man give the woman?

A. He gave her 15 dollars.

B. He changed her small fries into a medium.

C. He gave her a tip.

* burger〔'bɝgɚ〕*n.* 漢堡（= *hamburger*）

fries〔fraɪz〕*n. pl.* 薯條（= *French fries*）

medium〔'midɪəm〕*adj.* 中等的　　**orange juice** 柳橙汁

change〔tʃendʒ〕*n.* 零錢；找零　*v.* 改變

tip〔tɪp〕*n.* 小費

24. (**C**) W : Do you want to take some cake home for your brothers and sisters?

M : Thanks, but I'm an only child.

W : Really? I have three brothers.

Question : What does the boy mean?

A. He is too young to carry the cake.

B. There are four children in his family.

C. He has no brothers or sisters.

* *only child* 獨生子；獨生女　　mean〔min〕v. 意思是
carry〔'kærɪ〕v. 攜帶；拿

25. (**C**) M : Can I take a look at your paper?

W : Well, I'm not finished reading it yet.

M : I just want to take a quick look. I want to find out who won the game last night.

Question : What does the boy want?

A. He wants to copy the girl's homework.

B. He wants to watch the game.

C. He wants to look at the sports page.

* *take a look at* 看一眼
paper〔'pepə〕n. 報紙（= *newspaper*）
finished〔'fɪnɪʃt〕adj. 完成的
take a quick look 很快看一下　　*find out* 找出；查明
win〔wɪn〕v. 贏　　copy〔'kɑpɪ〕v. 抄襲
sports〔sports〕adj. 運動的　　page〔pedʒ〕n. 頁
sports page （報紙的）體育版

26. (**B**) W : Excuse me, is that clock right?

M : No. It runs a little fast.

W : Oh, good. I thought I was late for class.

Question : What does the boy mean?

A. The girl should run or she will be late for class.

B. The time shown on the clock is not correct.

C. The clock should speed up.

* right〔raɪt〕*adj.* 正確的

run〔rʌn〕*v.*（機器）運轉；跑

or〔ɔr〕*conj.* 否則   show〔ʃo〕*v.* 顯示

correct〔kə'rɛkt〕*adj.* 正確的   ***speed up*** 加速

27. (**C**) W : I called you last night, but you weren't at home.

M : I was at the library all evening.

W : What were you doing?

M : I was doing research for my history paper. I
didn't get home until 10:00.

Question : What was the man doing at 8:00 last night?

A. He was at the library.

B. He was making a telephone call.

C. He was doing homework.

* library〔'laɪ.brɛrɪ〕*n.* 圖書館

research〔'risɜtʃ , rɪ'sɜtʃ〕*n.* 研究

history〔'hɪstrɪ〕*n.* 歷史   paper〔'pepɚ〕*n.* 報告

not…until～ 直到～才…

make a telephone call 打電話

28. (**C**) M : Please take my seat.

W : Oh, I couldn't do that.

M : It's no problem. I'm getting off at the next stop.

W : Thank you.

Question : Where did this conversation take place?

A. In an airplane.

B. In a train station.

C. On a bus.

* ***take my seat*** 坐我的位子　　problem〔'prɑbləm〕*n.* 問題
  get off 下車 (↔ *get on*)　　***the next stop*** 下一站
  conversation〔ˌkɑnvə'seʃən〕*n.* 對話　　***take place*** 發生
  airplane〔'ɛrˌplen〕*n.* 飛機 (= *plane*)

29. (**B**) W : Which would you prefer, coffee or tea?

M : I usually drink coffee in the morning, but I think
I'll have tea for a change.

W : Here you are.

M : Thanks.

Question : Why does the man want to drink tea?

A. He always drinks tea in the morning.

B. He wants to do something different.

C. There is no more coffee.

* prefer〔prɪ'fɝ〕*v.* 比較喜歡　　***for a change*** 改變一下
  Here you are. 你要的東西在這裡；拿去吧。
  different〔'dɪfərənt〕*adj.* 不一樣的

30. (**A**) W：Have you started studying for the chemistry test yet?

M：No, not yet.

W：But the test is tomorrow!

M：That's all right. I always study for tests at the last minute.

Question：What does the boy mean?

A. He will study right before the test.

B. He will only study for one minute.

C. The test will start in one minute.

* chemistry〔'kɛmɪstrɪ〕n. 化學　　***not yet*** 尚未；還沒

That's all right. 沒關係。

at the last minute 在最後一刻　　right〔raɪt〕adv. 就在

二、閱讀能力測驗

第一部份：詞彙和結構

1. (**B**) Remember to close both the doors and the <u>windows</u> before you leave the classroom.

你離開教室之前，記得要關上門窗。

(A) light〔laɪt〕n. 燈

(B) ***window***〔'wɪndo〕n. 窗

(C) computer〔kəm'pjutə〕n. 電腦

(D) fan〔fæn〕n. 電扇

* (A)(C)(D) 皆為電器，「關掉」電器，須用 turn off，在此用法不合。　　remember〔rɪ'mɛmbə〕v. 記得

close〔kloz〕v. 關上

2. (**A**) When Mr. Lin is not home, there are usually several messages on the answering <u>machine</u>. 當林先生不在家的時候,電話答錄機上通常會有好幾個留言。

    (A) ***machine*** ﹝ məˈʃin ﹞ *n.* 機器
    answering machine 電話答錄機
    (B) telephone ﹝ˈtɛləˌfon ﹞ *n.* 電話
    (C) door ﹝ dor ﹞ *n.* 門
    (D) card ﹝ kɑrd ﹞ *n.* 卡片
    * several ﹝ˈsɛvərəl ﹞ *adj.* 好幾個
    message ﹝ˈmɛsɪdʒ ﹞ *n.* 留言;訊息

3. (**A**) After taking a bath, dry your body with a clean <u>towel</u>. 你洗完澡後,要用乾淨的<u>毛巾</u>擦乾身體。

    (A) ***towel*** ﹝ˈtauəl ﹞ *n.* 毛巾
    (B) tissue ﹝ˈtɪʃu ﹞ *n.* 衛生紙;面紙
    (C) toothbrush ﹝ˈtuθˌbrʌʃ ﹞ *n.* 牙刷
    (D) toothpaste ﹝ˈtuθˌpest ﹞ *n.* 牙膏
    * bath ﹝ bæθ ﹞ *n.* 洗澡   dry ﹝ draɪ ﹞ *v.* 擦乾
    clean ﹝ klin ﹞ *adj.* 乾淨的

4. (**C**) If you think the bus is going too fast, you may tell the <u>driver</u> to slow down. 如果你認為公車開太快,你可以告訴<u>司機</u>開慢一點。

    (A) teacher ﹝ˈtitʃɚ ﹞ *n.* 老師   (B) singer ﹝ˈsɪŋɚ ﹞ *n.* 歌手
    (C) ***driver*** ﹝ˈdraɪvɚ ﹞ *n.* 司機   (D) clerk ﹝ klɝk ﹞ *n.* 店員
    * go ﹝ go ﹞ *v.* 行進   ***slow down*** 慢下來;減速

5. (**D**) Sending <u>e-mail</u> is faster than writing a letter. More and more people are using it to write to their friends.

寄電子郵件比寫信快。有越來越多的人用它來寫信給朋友。

    (A) pen〔pɛn〕*n.* 筆

    (B) finger〔'fɪŋɚ〕*n.* 手指

    (C) communication〔kə,mjunə'keʃən〕*n.* 通訊；溝通

    (D) *e-mail*〔'i,mel〕*n.* 電子郵件

* send〔sɛnd〕*v.* 寄   *write to sb.* 寫信給某人

6. (**D**) Thank goodness the exams are <u>over</u>. We can relax now!

謝天謝地，考試結束了。我們現在可以輕鬆一下了！

sth. + *be* 動詞 + *over*   某事結束

* *thank goodness* 謝天謝地 (= *thank God*)

exam〔ɪg'zæm〕*n.* 考試   relax〔rɪ'læks〕*v.* 放輕鬆

7. (**B**) Be patient with your brother. <u>After all</u>, he is only three years old. 對你弟弟有耐心一點。畢竟，他只有三歲大。

    (A) at last 最後；終於   (B) *after all* 畢竟

    (C) at first 起初   (D) all the time 一直

* patient〔'peʃənt〕*adj.* 有耐心的

8. (**B**) The doctor told me <u>to take</u> the medicine three times a day.

醫生告訴我，要一天吃三次藥。

tell + *sb.* + *to V.* 告訴某人做～   take〔tek〕*v.* 吃藥

* medicine〔'mɛdəsn̩〕*n.* 藥   time〔taɪm〕*n.* 次數

9. (**A**) <u>Have</u> May and Edward told you the good news that we
won the basketball game?
梅和愛德華<u>有沒有</u>告訴你，我們贏得籃球比賽的好消息？

從 May and Edward 及 told 得知，空格應填助動詞
Have。而 (B) Has 用於單數主詞，(C) Did 及 (D) Do
後面須接原形動詞，故用法皆不合。

* news〔njuz〕*n.* 消息　　win〔wɪn〕*v.* 贏

10. (**C**) <u>Turn on</u> the radio and listen to the "English Garden"
program. <u>打開</u>收音機，並且收聽「英文花園」節目。

and 為對等連接詞，其後為原形動詞 listen，故空格亦須
填原形動詞，形成祈使句，故選 (C) **Turn on**「打開」。

* radio〔'redɪ,o〕*n.* 收音機　　**listen to** 收聽
garden〔'gardn̩〕*n.* 花園　　program〔'progræm〕*n.* 節目

11. (**A**) Did you notice Mother <u>wear</u> a new dress?
你有沒有注意到，媽媽<u>穿</u>新洋裝？

notice「注意到」的用法是：

notice + *sb.* + 原形 *V.* 注意到某人～

* dress〔drɛs〕*n.* 洋裝

12. (**B**) Mr. Wu makes much money <u>by</u> writing storybooks.
吳先生<u>靠</u>寫故事書，賺很多錢。

表「藉由～（方法）」，介系詞用 **by**。

* **make money** 賺錢　　storybook〔'storɪ,buk〕*n.* 故事書

13. (**A**) Paul often practices <u>speaking</u> English with the CD.
保羅經常利用 CD，來練習<u>說</u>英文。

> ***practice* + *V-ing*** 練習～

14. (**C**) George slipped on the floor, but he didn't hurt <u>himself</u>.
喬治在地板上滑倒，但是他並沒有<u>受傷</u>。

> ***hurt*** *oneself* 受傷
>
> * slip〔slɪp〕*v.* 滑倒　　floor〔flor〕*n.* 地板

15. (**A**) Tom hates studying history. He has no interest in
learning foreign languages <u>either</u>.
湯姆討厭研讀歷史。他對學習外語<u>也</u>沒興趣。

> 肯定句的「也」，用 too，否定句的「也」，須用 *either*。
>
> * hate〔het〕*v.* 討厭　　interest〔'ɪntrɪst〕*n.* 興趣 <*in*>
> foreign〔'fɔrɪn〕*adj.* 外國的
> language〔'læŋgwɪdʒ〕*n.* 語言

第二部份：段落填空

Questions 16-20

Many junior high students have started to look <u>for</u> their ideal
　　　　　　　　　　　　　　　　　　　　　　　　　16
boyfriends or girlfriends. Our teacher said it was not the right
time. She asked us to think about <u>why</u> we come to school.
　　　　　　　　　　　　　　　　　　17
"Studying is your most important job here," she said. "Also, you
may be too young <u>to solve</u> some problems."
　　　　　　　　　　18

很多國中生已經開始找尋他們心目中理想的異性朋友了。我們老師卻說,現在還不是時候。她要求我們想想,我們為何要上學。「唸書是你們在這裡最重要的事,」她說。「而且你們的年紀還小,沒辦法解決一些問題。」

ideal〔aɪ'diəl〕*adj.* 理想的　　right〔raɪt〕*adj.* 適當的

Then I asked my <u>seventeen-year-old</u> brother, David, about
                                19
this. He said, "Three years ago, I fell in love with a girl. I spent
most of my time <u>going</u> out with her. My grades became worse,
                        20
but my girlfriend still did well in her studies. So, it depends, I
think."

然後,我就問我十七歲的哥哥大衛這個問題。他說:「三年前,我和一個女孩子談戀愛。我花大部分的時間跟她出去。我的成績退步了,但是我的女朋友功課還是一樣很好。所以我覺得這要看情形而定。」

fall in love with *sb.* 與某人談戀愛
worse〔wɝs〕*adj.* 較差的(bad 的比較級)　　**_do well_** 表現好
studies〔'stʌdɪz〕*n. pl.* 學業　　depend〔dɪ'pɛnd〕*v.* 視⋯而定
It depends. 要看情況而定。

16. (**A**) 依句意,選 (A) **_look for_**「尋找」。而 (B) look into「調查」,(C) look out「小心」,(D) look in「往⋯裡面看」,均不合句意。

17. (**C**) 依句意,老師要我們想想看我們「為什麼」要上學,故用疑問詞 **_why_**,選 (C)。

18. (**B**) ***too…to V.*** 太…以致於不~
　　　solve (salv) *v.* 解決

19. (**D**) 表示「…歲的」的複合形容詞中，單位名詞須用單數。
　　　⎰ my seventeen-***year***-old brother
　　　⎱ = my brother who is seventeen ***years*** old

20. (**B**) 人 + ***spend*** + 時間 + ***V-ing*** （人）花時間做~
　　　go out 出去

Questions 21-25

Dear Steve,

　　I was pleased to get your letter. It reminds me of the happy days we <u>spent</u> together. As you know, I love nature.
　　　　　　　　　　21
Last week, I <u>took a trip</u> with my family to Yangmingshan
　　　　　　　　22
National Park. I saw many flowers there. The air <u>was full</u>
　　　　　　　　　　　　　　　　　　　　　23
<u>of</u> the singing of birds and the wonderful smell of flowers.

Along with this letter is a photo <u>taken</u> in front of a
　　　　　　　　　　　　　　　24
beautiful scenic spot. I'm sure <u>that</u> you'll agree it is very
　　　　　　　　　　　　　25
beautiful.

　　Remember me to your family.

　　　　　　　　　　　　　　With love,
　　　　　　　　　　　　　　Linda

親愛的史帝夫：

　　我很高興收到你的信。這讓我想到我們以前一起渡過的快樂時光。你知道我熱愛大自然。上星期我跟家人去陽明山國家公園。在那裡我看到很多花。空氣中充滿了鳥語花香。隨信附上一張在美麗景點前拍攝的照片。我想你一定也會同意這裡風景很美。

　　代我向你的家人問好。

　　　　　　　　　　　　　　　　　　愛你的
　　　　　　　　　　　　　　　　　　琳達

pleased〔plizd〕adj. 高興的
remind〔rɪ'maɪnd〕v. 提醒；使想起 < of >
nature〔'netʃɚ〕n. 大自然　　**national park** 國家公園
air〔ɛr〕n. 空氣　　singing〔'sɪŋɪŋ〕n.（鳥的）鳴叫
smell〔smɛl〕n. 味道　　**along with** 連同（= together with）
photo〔'foto〕n. 照片　　**in front of** 在…前面
scenic〔'sinɪk〕adj. 風景優美的　　spot〔spɑt〕n. 地點
sure〔ʃur〕adj. 確定的　　agree〔ə'gri〕v. 同意
remember sb. **to** ~ 代某人向~問候

21. (**A**) 依句意，我們一起「渡過」的快樂時光，「花費時間」用
　　　　spend 表示，故選 (A) **spent**。而 (B) take「花費時間」，
　　　　主詞須用人或事物，(C) cost「（東西）值~錢」，(D) start
　　　　「開始」，用法及句意均不合。

22. (**B**) **take a trip** 去旅行（= make a trip = go on a trip）

23. (**B**) **be full of** 充滿（= be filled with）
　　　　又 air 爲不可數名詞，故用單數動詞，選 (B) **was full of**。

24.(**C**) 依句意,附上一張在美麗景點前「被拍攝」的照片,故選 (C) ***taken***。

> ···is a photo ***taken*** in front of···
> = ···is a photo ***which was taken*** in front of···

25.(**D**)
> ***be sure of*** + *N.* 確信
> ***be sure that*** + 子句

空格後接的是主詞和動詞 you'll agree,因此是子句的

形式,故選 (D) ***that***。

第三部份:閱讀理解

Questions 26-27

阿囉哈海灘

一個享受陽光的絕佳地點!

規定:

1. 禁止划船。

2. 禁止釣魚。

3. 禁止升火。

4. 開放游泳時間:上午八點至晚上八點

5. 開放排球時間:下午兩點至五點

beach〔bitʃ〕*n.* 海灘　　great〔gret〕*adj.* 很棒的
sunshine〔'sʌn,ʃaɪn〕*n.* 陽光　　rule〔rul〕*n.* 規則
boat〔bot〕*v.* 划船　　fish〔fɪʃ〕*v.* 釣魚　　fire〔faɪr〕*n.* 火
hours〔aʊrz〕*n. pl.* 時間　　volleyball〔'vɑlɪ,bɔl〕*n.* 排球

26. (**C**) 在阿囉哈海灘，你可以做什麼？

       (A) 去划船。   (B) 生火烤肉。

       (C) <u>戲水。</u>   (D) 釣魚。

       * ***start a fire*** 生火（= *make a fire*）

       play with~ 玩~   barbecue〔'bɑrbɪ,kju〕*n.* 烤肉

27. (**B**) 如果你在晚上六點到阿囉哈海灘，你可以游泳和打排球嗎？

       (A) 兩者都不可以。

       (B) <u>你可以游泳，但是不能打排球。</u>

       (C) 你可以打排球，但是不能游泳。

       (D) 我們無法得知。

       * either〔'iðɚ〕*pron.*（兩者的）任一都不

Questions 28-29

速食快車

食品	價錢（新台幣）	飲料	價錢（新台幣）
熱狗	30	冰檸檬茶	25
起士漢堡	25	可樂 / 雪碧 / 芬達	20
牛肉三明治	40	熱咖啡	25
薯條	35	礦泉水	15
雞腿	40		
水果沙拉	50		

fast food 速食　　express〔ɪk'sprɛs〕*n.* 快車
price〔praɪs〕*n.* 價格　　drink〔drɪŋk〕*n.* 飲料
hot dog 熱狗　　cheeseburger〔'tʃiz,bɝɡɚ〕*n.* 起士漢堡
beef〔bif〕*n.* 牛肉　　sandwich〔'sændwɪtʃ〕*n.* 三明治
drumstick〔'drʌm,stɪk〕*n.* 雞腿　　salad〔'sæləd〕*n.* 沙拉
iced〔aɪst〕*adj.* 冰的　　lemon〔'lɛmən〕*n.* 檸檬
mineral〔'mɪnərəl〕*adj.* 礦物的　　*mineral water* 礦泉水

28. (**D**) 哪一種食物跟飲料加起來最貴？

(A) 薯條和可樂。【35 + 20 = 55（元）】
(B) 牛肉三明治和雪碧。【40 + 20 = 60（元）】
(C) 起士漢堡和冰檸檬茶。【25 + 25 = 50（元）】
(D) 水果沙拉和礦泉水。【50 + 15 = 65（元）】

29. (**D**) 海倫不吃肉。她能買什麼？

(A) 熱狗。
(B) 雞腿。
(C) 牛肉三明治。
(D) 水果沙拉。

* meat〔mit〕*n.* 肉

Questions 30-31

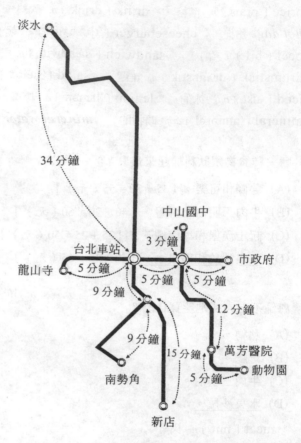

淡水

34 分鐘

中山國中

台北車站   3 分鐘

龍山寺   5 分鐘   市政府

5 分鐘   5 分鐘

9 分鐘   12 分鐘

9 分鐘   萬芳醫院

15 分鐘   動物園

南勢角   5 分鐘

新店

30. (**A**)　楊氏一家人要去台北市立動物園看無尾熊及企鵝。他們要從市
　　　　　政府站搭捷運。到台北市立動物園要花多久時間？

　　　　　(A) <u>至少二十二分鐘。</u>　　　(B) 至少十七分鐘。

　　　　　(C) 至少十二分鐘。　　　　(D) 至少十分鐘。

　　　　　* koala〔koˋɑlə〕n. 無尾熊　　penguin〔ˋpɛngwɪn〕n. 企鵝
　　　　　　at least 至少
　　　　　　市政府站 → 忠孝復興站 → 動物園站：5 + 12 + 5 = 22（分鐘）

31. (**B**) 海倫想和家人去淡水。到達那裡要花他們大約三十九分鐘的
時間。他們現在人在哪裡？

(A) 中山國中站。【中山國中站 → 忠孝復興站 → 台北火車站
→ 淡水站：3 + 5 + 34 = 41（分鐘），不合。】

(B) 龍山寺站。【龍山寺站 → 台北火車站 → 淡水站：5 + 34 =
39（分鐘）】

(C) 市政府站。【市政府站 → 忠孝復興站 → 台北火車站 →
淡水站：5 + 5 + 34 = 44（分鐘），不合。】

(D) 台北火車站。【台北火車站 → 淡水站：34（分鐘），
不合。】

Questions 32-34

Take a walk through some woods where trees have just been cut down, and look at the stumps（殘株）of these trees. You will see many little rings in the center, then larger ones, and still larger ones. Count these rings. Trees grow a ring each year. So if a tree has twenty rings, it is twenty years old. Next time you see the stump of a tree that has just been cut down, try to tell how old the tree was.

在有樹剛被砍伐的森林中散步，看看這些樹的殘株。你會看到中央有許多小小的圓圈，然後會有較大圈的，再來就是更大圈的。數一數這些年輪。每年樹的年輪都會增加一圈。所以如果一棵樹有二十圈年輪，那它就有二十歲了。下次你看到剛被砍下的樹的殘株的時候，試著判斷這棵樹的樹齡。

take a walk 去散步　　through〔θru〕*prep.* 通過；穿過

woods〔wʊdz〕*n. pl.* 森林　　just〔dʒʌst〕*adv.* 剛剛

cut down 砍伐　　stump〔stʌmp〕*n.* 樹被砍倒後留下的殘株

ring〔rɪŋ〕*n.* 圓圈；（樹木的）年輪

center〔'sɛntɚ〕*n.* 中央　　still〔stɪl〕*adv.* 還要大

count〔kaʊnt〕*v.* 數　　grow〔gro〕*v.* 生長；長出

next time 下一次　　tell〔tɛl〕*v.* 判斷

32. (**A**) 本文告訴我們如何看出樹的

(A) 年齡。　　　　　　　(B) 大小。

(C) 重量。　　　　　　　(D) 高度。

* reading〔'ridɪŋ〕*n.* 文章　　age〔edʒ〕*n.* 年齡
size〔saɪz〕*n.* 尺寸；大小　　weight〔wet〕*n.* 重量
height〔haɪt〕*n.* 高度

33. (**D**) 樹的年齡是藉由看樹的 ＿＿＿＿＿＿＿ 得知。

(A) 葉子　　　　　　　　(B) 樹皮

(C) 根　　　　　　　　　(D) 殘株

* learn〔lɝn〕*v.* 知道
leaf〔lif〕*n.* 葉子（leaves 爲複數形）
bark〔bɑrk〕*n.* 樹皮　　root〔rut〕*n.*（植物的）根

34. (**A**) 何者爲眞？

(A) 有七個年輪的樹木已經活了七年。

(B) 一棵二十歲的樹會有二十多個年輪。

(C) 樹的年輪數目是由它吸收了多少水份來決定。

(D) 不同種類的樹會用不同的方式來表現其年齡。

* ***more than*** 超過（= *over*）
number〔'nʌmbɚ〕*n.* 數目　　decide〔dɪ'saɪd〕*v.* 決定
kind〔kaɪnd〕*n.* 種類　　way〔we〕*n.* 方式

Question 35

參觀者須持票
才能進入

visitor〔'vɪzɪtə〕n. 參觀者　　enter〔'ɛntə〕v. 進入
without〔wɪð'aʊt〕prep. 沒有
ticket〔'tɪkɪt〕n. 門票；入場券；罰單

35. (**A**)　這個告示牌是什麼意思？

(A) 想進入的人必須持有入場券。

(B) 想參觀的人進入售票處。

(C) 想買門票的人進入此門。

(D) 參觀的人可能會收到警察開的違規停車的罰單。

* sign〔saɪn〕n. 告示牌　　mean〔min〕v. 意思是
　hold〔hold〕v. 擁有　　visit〔'vɪzɪt〕v. 參觀；遊覽
　ticket office 售票處
　parking ticket 違規停車的罰單
　the police 警方

三、寫作能力測驗

第一部份：單句寫作

第 1～5 題：句子改寫

1. My boyfriend cooked me some spaghetti.

   My boyfriend _____ me.

   重點結構：cook 的用法

   解　答：<u>My boyfriend cooked some spaghetti for me.</u>

   句型分析：cook + 直接受詞（物）+ for + 間接受詞（人）

   說　明：「為某人煮東西」有兩種寫法：「cook + *sb.* + *sth.*」或「cook + *sth.* + for + *sb.*」，這題要改成第二種用法，先寫物（some spaghetti），再寫介系詞 for，再接人（me）。

   * spaghetti〔spə'gɛtɪ〕*n.* 義大利麵

2. Cartoons are interesting to most children.

   Most children are _____ cartoons.

   重點結構：「be 動詞 + interested + in」的用法

   解　答：<u>Most children are interested in cartoons.</u>

   句型分析：主詞 + be 動詞 + interested + in + 受詞

   說　明：動詞 interest「使感興趣」的形容詞有兩個，一個是現在分詞 interesting，一個是過去分詞 interested，其用法為：

   　事物 + be 動詞 + interesting + to + 人
   　人 + be 動詞 + interested + in + 事物

   本題的主詞是 Most children，故用形容詞 interested。

   * cartoon〔kɑr'tun〕*n.* 卡通影片

3. Tina went to the swimming school.

When _____?

重點結構：過去式的 wh-問句

解　答：<u>When did Tina go to the swimming school?</u>

句型分析：When + did + 主詞 + 原形動詞？

説　明：這一題應將過去式直述句改爲 wh-問句，除了要加
　　　　助動詞 did，還要記得助動詞後面的動詞，須用原
　　　　形動詞，因此 went 要改成 go。

* *swimming school* 游泳訓練班

4. To keep it a secret may be a good idea.

It _____.

重點結構：以 It 爲虛主詞引導的句子

解　答：<u>It may be a good idea to keep it a secret.</u>

句型分析：It + 助動詞 + 動詞 + 名詞 + 不定詞

説　明：虛主詞 It 代替不定詞片語，不定詞片語 to keep it a
　　　　secret 才是眞正的主詞，須置於句尾。

* keep〔kip〕*v.* 使停留在…狀態
　secret〔ˋsikrɪt〕*n.* 秘密　　*keep it a secret* 保密

5. The Greens bought that house last week.

That house _____ last week.

重點結構：被動語態字序

解　答：<u>That house was bought by the Greens last week.</u>

句型分析：主詞 + be 動詞 + 過去分詞 + by + 受詞

説　明：被動語態的形式是「be 動詞 + 過去分詞」，故動詞
　　　　bought 須改爲 was bought。

第 6～10 題：句子合併

6. I saw my brother in the living room.

My brother was watching TV.

I saw ＿＿＿＿＿＿＿＿＿＿＿＿ in the living room.

　　重點結構：see 的用法

　　　解　答：I saw my brother watch TV in the living room.

　　　　　或 I saw my brother watching TV in the living room.

　　句型分析：主詞＋動詞＋受詞＋原形動詞或現在分詞

　　　說　明：see 的用法：

$$\begin{cases} \text{see ＋ 受詞 ＋ 原形動詞（表主動）} \\ \text{see ＋ 受詞 ＋ 現在分詞（表主動進行）} \end{cases}$$

7. This postcard is pretty.

That postcard is pretty.

This postcard ＿＿＿＿＿＿＿＿＿ as that postcard.

　　　重點結構：「as…as～」的用法

　　　　解　答：This postcard is as pretty as that postcard.

　　　句型分析：主詞＋be 動詞＋as＋形容詞＋as＋受詞

　　　　說　明：這題是說這兩張照片都很漂亮，用「as…as～」

　　　　　　　　來連接兩句，表「和～一樣…」。

　　＊ postcard〔'post,kɑrd〕n. 明信片

　　　pretty〔'prɪtɪ〕adj. 漂亮的

8. We have to walk fast.
   We want to catch the train.
   Walk fast, or _____ will not _____.

   重點結構：or 的用法
   解　答：<u>Walk fast, or we will not catch the train.</u>
   句型分析：原形動詞, or + 主詞 + 動詞
   説　明：這題的意思是說「走快點，不然我們就趕不上火車了」，連接詞 or 表「否則」。
   * catch〔kætʃ〕v. 趕上

9. I have been reading a novel.
   I just finished it two days ago.
   I just finished _____.

   重點結構：finish 的用法
   解　答：<u>I just finished (reading) a novel two days ago.</u>
   句型分析：主詞 + 動詞 + (動) 名詞 + 時間副詞
   説　明：finish (完成) 的用法是後面接名詞或動名詞做受詞，故有兩種寫法：finished a novel 或 finished reading a novel。
   * novel〔ˈnɑvḷ〕n. 小說

10. My dog is smart.

My dog is cute.

My dog is not only _____.

重點結構：「not only…but (also)～」的用法

解　答：My dog is not only smart but (also) cute.

句型分析：主詞 + be 動詞 + not only + 形容詞 + but (also) + 形容詞

說　明：這題的意思是說「我的小狗既聰明又可愛」，用「not only…but (also)～」來連接兩句，表「不但～而且…」。

第 11～15 題：重組

11. Do you know _____?

when / plane / take / the / off / will

重點結構：「Do you know + when + 主詞 + 動詞」的用法

解　答：Do you know when the plane will take off?

句型分析：Do you know + 疑問詞 + 主詞 + 動詞？

說　明：when 引導名詞子句，做動詞 know 的受詞。

* plane〔plen〕n. 飛機　　*take off* 起飛

12. Which _____, black or white?

like / color / you / better / do

重點結構：wh-問句的用法

解　答：Which color do you like better, black or white?

句型分析：Which + 名詞 + 助動詞 + 主詞 + 動詞？

說　明：本句的意思是「你比較喜歡哪一個顏色，黑色或白色？」即問句的形式，先寫助動詞，再寫主詞。

13. It's ＿＿＿＿＿＿＿＿＿＿＿＿＿＿＿＿＿＿＿＿＿＿＿.

impossible / near / to find / a / almost / parking space
/ our school

重點結構：以 It 為虛主詞引導的句子

解　答：<u>It's almost impossible to find a parking space
near our school.</u>

句型分析：It's + 形容詞 + 不定詞

說　明：虛主詞 It 代替不定詞片語，不定詞片語 to find a
parking space near our school 才是真正的主詞，
須置於句尾。副詞 almost 修飾形容詞 impossible。

* almost〔'ɔl,most〕adv. 幾乎
impossible〔ɪm'pɑsəbļ〕adj. 不可能的
space〔spes〕n. 空位　　*parking space* 停車位

14. How ＿＿＿＿＿＿＿＿＿＿＿＿＿＿＿＿＿＿＿＿?

you / would / your / like / steak

重點結構：wh-問句的用法

解　答：<u>How would you like your steak?</u>

句型分析：How + 助動詞 + 主詞 + 動詞？

說　明：本句是問「你的牛排要幾分熟？」即問句的形式，先
寫助動詞，再寫主詞。

* steak〔stek〕n. 牛排

15. Robert _____.

come / this evening / will / to / visit / us

> 重點結構：「主詞＋助動詞＋動詞」的用法
>
> 解　答：<u>Robert will come to visit us this evening.</u>
>
> 句型分析：主詞＋助動詞＋動詞
>
> 說　明：這題有三個動詞 come、will 和 visit，助動詞 will
> 　　　　須擺在最前面，後面接原形動詞 come，visit 前面
> 　　　　加 to，形成不定詞，表目的，故本句的意思是「羅
> 　　　　伯特今晚將來拜訪我們」。

第二部份：段落寫作

題目：昨天是中秋節（Mid-Autumn Festival），請根據圖片內容寫一
　　　篇約 50 字的簡短描述。

Yesterday was the Mid-Autumn Festival.　My family and I had a barbecue outside.　We ate meat and bread.　*After* we ate, my mother told us a story.　She told us about Chang O, the lady in the moon.　She drank a magical drink, and then flew to the moon.　She still lives there.

After the story, we looked at the moon.　The moon was full. We ate a lot of moon cakes.　We all had a good time *last night*.

mid- 〔mɪd〕中間的（用於複合字）

autumn 〔'ɔtəm〕 *n.* 秋天　　festival 〔'fɛstəvḷ〕 *n.* 節日

Mid-Autumn Festival 中秋節

outside 〔'aʊt'saɪd〕 *adv.* 在戶外

bread 〔brɛd〕 *n.* 麵包　　*Chang O* 嫦娥

lady 〔'ledɪ〕 *n.* 女士；小姐　　moon 〔mun〕 *n.* 月亮

magical 〔'mædʒɪkḷ〕 *adj.* 有魔力的；神奇的

fly 〔flaɪ〕 *v.* 飛（三態變化爲：fly-flew-flown）

look at 看　　full 〔fʊl〕 *adj.* 滿月的

moon cake 月餅　　*have a good time* 玩得愉快

附錄

全民英語能力分級檢定測驗簡介

「全民英語能力分級檢定測驗」（General English Proficiency Test），簡稱「全民英檢」（GEPT），旨在提供我國各階段英語學習者一公平、可靠、具效度之英語能力評量工具，測驗對象包括在校學生及一般社會人士，可做為學習成果檢定、教學改進及公民營機構甄選人才等之參考。

本測驗為標準參照測驗（criterion-referenced test），參考當前我國英語教育體制，制定分級標準，整套系統共分五級——初級（Elementary）、中級（Intermediate）、中高級（High-Intermediate）、高級（Advanced）、優級（Superior）。每級訂有明確能力標準（詳見表一綜合能力說明），報考者可依英語能力選擇適當級數報考，每級均包含聽、說、讀、寫四項完整的測驗，通過所報考級數的能力標準即可取得該級的合格證書。各級命題設計均參考目前各階段英語教育之課程大綱及相關教材之內容分析，期能符合國內各階段英語教育的需求、反應本土的生活經驗與特色。

「全民英語能力檢定分級測驗」各級綜合能力說明　　《表一》

級數	綜　合　能　力	備　　　　註	
初級	通過初級測驗者具有基礎英語能力，能理解和使用淺易日常用語，英語能力相當於國中畢業者。	建議下列人員宜具有該級英語能力	一般行政助理、維修技術人員、百貨業、餐飲業、旅館業或觀光景點服務人員、計程車駕駛等。
中級	通過中級測驗者具有使用簡單英語進行日常生活溝通的能力，英語能力相當於高中職畢業者。		一般行政、業務、技術、銷售人員、護理人員、旅館、飯店接待人員、總機人員、警政人員、旅遊從業人員等。
中高級	通過中高級測驗者英語能力逐漸成熟，應用的領域擴大，雖有錯誤，但無礙溝通，英語能力相當於大學非英語主修系所畢業者。		商務、企劃人員、祕書、工程師、研究助理、空服人員、航空機師、航管人員、海關人員、導遊、外事警政人員、新聞從業人員、資訊管理人員等。

級數	綜　合　能　力		備　　　　註
高級	通過高級測驗者英語流利順暢，僅有少許錯誤，應用能力擴及學術或專業領域，英語能力相當於國內大學英語主修系所或曾赴英語系國家大學或研究所進修並取得學位者。	建議下列人員宜具有該級英語能力	高級商務人員、協商談判人員、英語教學人員、研究人員、翻譯人員、外交人員、國際新聞從業人員等。
優級	通過優級測驗者的英語能力接近受過高等教育之母語人士，各種場合均能使用適當策略作最有效的溝通。		專業翻譯人員、國際新聞特派人員、外交官員、協商談判主談人員等。

初級英語能力測驗簡介

I. 通過初級檢定者的英語能力

聽	說	讀	寫
能聽懂簡易的英語句子、對話及故事。	能簡單地自我介紹並以簡易英語對答；能朗讀簡易文章。	能瞭解簡易英語對話、短文、故事及書信的內容；能看懂常用的標示。	能寫簡單的英語句子及段落。

II. 測　驗　內　容

測驗項目	初　試			複　試
	聽力測驗	閱讀能力測驗	寫作能力測驗	口說能力測驗
總題數	30	35	16	18
作答時間 / 分鐘	約 20	35	40	約 10
測驗內容	看圖辨義 問答 簡短對話	詞彙和結構 段落填空 閱讀理解	單句寫作 段落寫作	複誦 朗讀句子與短文 回答問題

　　聽力及閱讀能力測驗成績採標準計分方式，60 分爲平均數，滿分 120 分。寫作及口說能力測驗成績採整體式評分，使用級分制，分爲 0～5 級分，再轉換成百分制。各項成績通過標準如下：

III. 成績計算及通過標準

初　試	通過標準 / 滿分	複　試	通過標準 / 滿分
聽力測驗 閱讀能力測驗 寫作能力測驗	80 / 120 分 80 / 120 分 70 / 100 分	口說能力測驗	80 / 100 分

IV. 寫作能力測驗級分説明

第一部份：單句寫作級分説明

級　分	説　　　明
2	正確無誤。
1	有誤，但重點結構正確。
0	錯誤過多、未答、等同未答。

第二部份：段落寫作級分説明

級　分	説　　　明
5	正確表達題目之要求；文法、用字等幾乎無誤。
4	大致正確表達題目之要求；文法、用字等有誤，但不影響讀者之理解。
3	大致回答題目之要求，但未能完全達意；文法、用字等有誤，稍影響讀者之理解。
2	部份回答題目之要求，表達上有令人不解/誤解之處；文法、用字等皆有誤，讀者須耐心解讀。
1	僅回答1個問題或重點；文法、用字等錯誤過多，嚴重影響讀者之理解。
0	未答、等同未答。

各部份題型之題數、級分及總分計算公式：

分項測驗	測驗題型	各部份題數	每題級分	佔總分比重
第一部份：單句寫作	A. 句子改寫	5題	2分	50 ％
	B. 句子合併	5題	2分	
	C. 重組	5題	2分	
第二部份：段落寫作	看圖表寫作	1篇	5分	50 ％
總分計算公式	公式：{(第一部份得分/30)＋(第二部份得分/5)}×50 例：第一部份各項得分 A－8分 　　　　　　　　　　　　B－10分 　　　　　　　　　　　　C－8分 8+10+8=26 三項加總第一部份得分 － 26分 第二部份得分 － 4分 依公式計算如下： {(26/30)＋(4/5)}×50=83　該考生得分83分			

　　凡應考且合乎規定者一律發給成績單。初試及複試各項測驗成績通過者，發給合格證書，本測驗成績紀錄保存兩年。

　　初試通過者，可於一年內單獨報考複試，得重複報考。惟複試一旦通過，即不得再報考。

　　已通過本英檢測驗初級，一年內不得再報考同級數之測驗。違反本規定報考者，其應試資格將被取消，且不退費。

（以上資料取自「全民英檢學習網站」http://www.gept.org.tw）

初級英語檢定模考班

　　21世紀是證照的時代，一般服務業，如行政助理、百貨業、餐飲業、旅館業、觀光景點服務人員及計程車駕駛等，均須通過此項測驗。

　　「初級英語檢定測驗」初試項目包含①聽力測驗－分為看圖辨義、問答、簡短對話三部分。②閱讀能力測驗－分為詞彙和結構、段落填空、閱讀理解三部分。③寫作能力測驗－包含單句寫作及段落寫作二部分。

- **招生目的**：協助同學通過「初級英語檢定測驗」。

- **招生對象**：任何人均可以參加。通過初級測驗者具有基礎英語能力，能理解和使用淺易日常用語。

- **上課時間**：每週日下午 2:00 ～ 5:00（共八週）

- **收費標準**：4800 元（劉毅英文家教班學生僅收 3800 元）

- **上課內容**：完全比照財團法人語言訓練中心所做「初級英語檢定測驗」初試標準。分為聽力測驗、閱讀能力測驗，及寫作能力測驗三部分。每次上課舉行 70 分鐘的模擬考，包含 30 題聽力測驗，35 題詞彙結構、段落填空、閱讀理解、及 15 題單句寫作、及一篇段落寫作。考完試後立即講解，馬上釐清所有問題。

劉毅英文家教班（國一、國二、國三、高一、高二、高三班）

班址：台北市重慶南路一段 10 號 7 F（火車站前‧日盛銀行樓上）

電話：(02) 2381-3148‧2331-8822　　網址：www.learnschool.com.tw

||||||||||||||| ● 學習出版公司門市部 ● |||||||||||||||

台北地區：台北市許昌街 10 號 2 樓　TEL：(02)2331-4060・2331-9209
台中地區：台中市綠川東街 32 號 8 樓 23 室
　　　　　TEL：(04)2223-2838

|||||||||||||||||||||||||||||||||||||||||||||||||

初級英檢模擬試題②

主　　　編／林 銀 姿
發 行 所／學習出版有限公司　　　☎ (02) 2704-5525
郵 撥 帳 號／0512727-2 學習出版社帳戶
登 記 證／局版台業 2179 號
印 刷 所／裕強彩色印刷有限公司
台 北 門 市／台北市許昌街 10 號 2 F　　☎ (02) 2331-4060・2331-9209
台 中 門 市／台中市綠川東街 32 號 8 F 23 室　　☎ (04) 2223-2838
台灣總經銷／紅螞蟻圖書有限公司　　☎ (02) 2795-3656
美國總經銷／Evergreen Book Store　☎ (818) 2813622
本公司網址　www.learnbook.com.tw
電 子 郵 件　learnbook@learnbook.com.tw

售價：新台幣二百二十元正

2006 年 1 月 1 日一版三刷

ISBN 957-519-664-3